I0574769

HER COWBOY BILLIONAIRE BACHELOR

CHRISTMAS IN CORAL CANYON, AN EVERETT SISTERS NOVEL, BOOK 6

LIZ ISAACSON

Copyright © 2018 by Elana Johnson, writing as Liz Isaacson

All rights reserved.

No part of this book may be reproduced in any form or by any electronic or mechanical means, including information storage and retrieval systems, without written permission from the author, except for the use of brief quotations in a book review.

ISBN-13: 978-1-63876-163-1

CHAPTER 1

Rose Everett waited in the airport, almost desperate for her flight number to be called. Her stomach felt like it was going to claw itself out, but there was nothing she could do. She told herself that over and over again.

There's nothing you can do. There's nothing you can do.

Rose had quite a large skill-set, but flying a plane wasn't included.

Her oldest sister, Lily, had called that morning. Her blood pressure was off the charts, and she'd been hospitalized. She'd asked Rose to come help her get the nursery ready, as she wasn't due for another eight weeks. The medication she'd been given seemed to be working fine, but she'd be staying in the hospital overnight.

Always the worrier of the sisters, Rose glanced toward the gate again. The attendant worked there, but Rose wondered what he was really doing. Probably checking email or social media.

Rose couldn't wait to meet her new nephew. It would be the first baby in the Everett family, and she'd been trying to get Lily to name the boy Wally for four months. Lily didn't like the sound of Wally Whittaker, but it made Rose smile every time she thought of it.

And Lily and Beau didn't have a name picked out yet anyway. Everything Rose suggested was tossed away as if Jeremy and Evan were the worst names in the world.

She should be secretly glad that Lily disliked everything she suggested. Then she could use Wally for her son—if she ever got married. Or met a man with a last name that started with a W.

All the Whittaker men were spoken for now, so she'd have to hunt for someone else.

Nope, she thought, shooting the gate attendant another look. Didn't he know they were supposed to start boarding fifteen minutes ago? Rose wanted to march over there and demand he do something. But she kept her diva card safely in her pocket. A few people had cast her glances, but for the most part, she'd hidden successfully behind her phone.

Rose secretly hoped she could stay in Coral Canyon for a while. Lily had lived there for a couple of years now. And Vi had just gone back a few months ago. They'd both found the perfect cowboys for them, and Rose couldn't help thinking that maybe she could too. Maybe she and her sisters could keep recording albums from Wyoming instead of Nashville.

It was probably a fool's hope. But Rose clung to it, because she didn't have anything else. She'd given away her chinchilla to take this trip. And she'd been through a string of men in the past eight or nine months that had left her wondering what the point was.

Yes, she had her parents in Nashville, but her mother had even started talking about moving to Coral Canyon to be closer to Lily and Vi—and her new grandson. Rose wasn't so blind that she didn't know the real reason her parents would uproot themselves from the city they'd lived in for almost twenty years. Well, at least when her father wasn't traveling overseas.

And it was the same reason she currently sat in the airport.

That baby. Oh, how she loved that baby, and he hadn't even been born yet.

Rose didn't want to be left behind. Again. So if she got to Coral Canyon first….

That was the story of her life. Always last. Last to know important things. Last to come into the Everett family. Last to get her opinion asked. And of course, it had happened again in her love life.

Finally, her flight number was called, and those needing special assistance were invited to come forward. Rose didn't need special assistance, but she did have a first-class ticket and she needed to stretch her back. As she did, she scoped out the other people in the waiting area. She wasn't sure what she was looking for, but she liked people-watching. She wondered what each person's story was. Where they came from. Where they were going. Maybe they were traveling to see loved ones. Or maybe they were headed home after a visit.

She caught a young mother's eye, and smiled before she looked away to collect her purse and carryon bag.

She wasn't sure why people fascinated her so much, but she knew she liked imagining them whenever she sat down to write songs. After all, country music was about people. People, and the people they loved.

"We now welcome our first-class passengers to flight 6234."

Relief spread through Rose and she wheeled her bag toward the gate. A scan, a smile, and a few steps and she was on the plane. Finally. She deliberately booked the second row in first class, so she'd have somewhere to put her things under the seat in front of her. It was the best of both worlds, and anyone who traveled as much as she did knew it.

She had a window seat, and she was glad to let the man behind her heave her suitcase into the overhead bin before getting out of the way. She picked up the pillow and blanket left on her seat and sat down. She buckled her seatbelt, even though the flight wouldn't take off for a good twenty minutes.

The bottle of water next to her separated her and the passenger who'd have the aisle seat. But no one came. The flight attendant kept saying their flight was full and that larger carry-on items would need to be tagged and picked up at the gate in Jackson Hole. And still, no one took the seat beside her.

Just when she thought she'd have a stress-free, no-small-talk flight, a man appeared in the aisle. He had no baggage. Not even a backpack. Just his phone and his wallet, which he shoved in his back pocket. He was clean-shaven, with a nice jawline and the most dazzling pair of aqua eyes Rose had ever seen. Surely he was wearing fake contacts to make his eyes that color. It was like looking into the ocean while the sun lit it up.

"I'm right here," he said, sliding into his seat.

Rose couldn't say anything. He smelled like pine trees and fresh rain, and she wondered where he'd been. Certainly not in that waiting area. Rose would've definitely seen him.

He buckled up as the flight attendants started going over the safety procedures. He'd been one of the very last people on the plane, and it didn't seem to bother him at all. Rose watched him out of the corner of her eye, hoping she wasn't being too obvious.

She already had her headphones plugged into her phone, and the music playing. She had one earbud in and the other draped over her ear as she pretended to listen to the flight attendants talk about a water landing.

The gorgeous stranger next to her didn't seem to care about the demonstration. He turned his head toward her and said, "Are you staying in Wyoming when we get there?"

Oh, so he was one of *those* kind of people. One who'd want to talk for the whole three-hour flight. Despite his stunning looks, Rose wasn't interested in that. No, thank you.

"For a bit," she said evasively. She did not ask him the same question, though curiosity touched her mind. Maybe if he was in town, they could—

She cut the thought off. Coral Canyon was an hour's drive

from Jackson Hole, where they were flying into. He wouldn't be staying anywhere near her.

And she wasn't interested anyway.

"What are you doing there?" he asked.

She glared at him, but he'd clearly endured such things before, because it didn't ruffle him in the slightest. Oh, boy. One of *those* people.

"My sister is going to have her baby soon."

"Oh, fantastic." His beautiful teeth made an appearance as he smiled. Rose got stuck on the movement of his lips, forgetting to be annoyed with him for a moment. "Boy or girl?"

"Boy," she said. "She's having trouble with her blood pressure." Why she'd said that, she wasn't sure. She'd had plenty of experience making small talk with strangers, and she'd learned from the time she was twelve not to engage them if she didn't want to keep talking.

"Is she on Labetalol?" He looked at her with genuine interest in those eyes.

Rose blinked. "Was that English?"

He chuckled and glanced at the flight attendant. "It was, though I can say it in Spanish, Portuguese, and Swahili."

Rose rolled her eyes then and looked out the window. He was one of *those* people. Someone who had to let everyone know how freaking smart they were.

No, thank you.

She put in her second earbud and pressed up the volume on her phone though the flight attendant hadn't finished with the instructions should they need to make an emergency landing. She didn't care. She'd flown hundreds of times, and today wasn't going to be the day the plane crashed.

Rose closed her eyes and tried not to breathe in too deeply. Then she wouldn't be reminded of the handsome man beside her and do something insane—like talk to him.

———

Rose woke to a delightfully warm hand on her arm. She startled, first looking into that pair of clear, teal eyes, and then dropping her gaze to where the man's hand still rested on her arm.

His mouth moved, but she couldn't hear him over the pounding music coming through her headphones. How she'd fallen asleep, she had no idea. She practically ripped the earbuds out of her ears and asked, "What?"

It was more of a yell, really. Embarrassment heated her, as if she wasn't already warm enough from being asleep.

"Do you have a bag?" he asked, his voice somehow deeper than before. Or maybe Rose was still trying to throw off the dregs of slumber.

"Yes," she said. "It's right above us. It's black."

It's black. She shook her head. Ninety-nine percent of the traveling population had a black bag.

"It has a rose on the top," she said.

"This one?" He hefted her bag to the aisle.

"That's it." She stepped out behind him, wondering if he was going to take her personal belongings hostage. But once they were in the jetway, he handed her the bag.

"Why the rose?" he asked.

"Um, that's my name," she said. "Rose."

Their eyes met again, and if he couldn't feel that electricity between them, he'd have to be dead. Rose felt tingly from head to toe, as if she'd been struck by lightning.

"Nice to meet you, Rose. I'm Liam." He extended his hand, and she thankfully had enough brain cells to put her hand in his. My, his skin felt nice and smooth and warm....

She blinked and gave him a proper handshake. She didn't want to be the dazed woman with a limp noodle shake.

"Nice nails," he said as he released her hand. "Are they real?"

"Yes," she said, glancing at her fingernails. She adored getting her nails done, and today, they were bright pink to match the lipstick she'd been favoring this month. After all, it was almost Valentine's Day—in another month—and the holiday practically screamed for pink.

He walked ahead of her, and though Rose worked out regularly, she couldn't quite catch him. Once they made it into the airport in Jackson Hole, he turned, smiled, and said, "Maybe we'll run into each other again."

"Maybe," she said, the second syllable falling into open space as Liam walked away from her, a wave over his shoulder. He was obviously off to somewhere very important.

Someone probably needs a Swahili translator, she thought with a scoff, still watching him weave through the crowd. In fact, she stood there watching him in his pressed cotton pants and black polo until he disappeared.

"Liam," she said to herself. One of her greatest skills was Googling for information, but even she couldn't do much with only a first name.

But she wasn't going to let that stop her from trying.

Liam intrigued her, and she wanted her "maybe" to become a "definitely."

Oh, yes, she *definitely* wanted to run into Liam again.

CHAPTER 2

Liam Murphy practically ran through the airport, wondering what Rose thought of his sudden and quick departure. *Doesn't matter*, he told himself. He'd likely never see her again, even if he found her one of the most beautiful people he'd ever encountered.

So she had a cold shoulder on the plane. A lot of people did, Liam found. He wasn't one of them, and he loved talking to people, learning about them, experiencing their lives.

He probably should've kept the medical lingo under his tongue. She'd seemed put off by that. No, it was the bragging about the languages. Whatever it was, she'd stuck in her headphones and fallen asleep about five minutes after take-off.

Which was fine with Liam, because it had been a long few days of getting back to the United States. He was almost there. Almost home.

He didn't think for a moment that his parents would be waiting for him outside security. No, he'd have a driver, holding a sign with his name on it, and the last thing he wanted was for Rose to see that. The Murphy money could buy a lot, and Liam liked to keep it on the down-low.

Sure enough, he went down the escalator and found the man

in the crisp, black suit standing there with the placard. He almost rolled his eyes. He knew how to get a taxi, or rent a car, or even bum a ride. This was Jackson Hole for crying out loud, and that guy looked like he was picking up the President of the United States.

"Hey," Liam said, noticing a group of people to his right. A woman with short blonde hair stood with a cowboy, and there were at least a dozen more people gathered around. But not really.

Liam had spent his life observing people—usually for symptoms that would tell him something—but he was particularly good at seeing things. And those people weren't with the man and woman, but they were definitely interested in them.

"Where is she?" the woman asked. "I swear her flight should be here by now."

"Didn't you say Rose was always late?" the cowboy asked.

Liam sucked in a breath and spun back toward the escalators that led down from the second floor. He didn't see Rose, but everything in him wanted to. He turned back to the driver. "Let's go."

"You're ready?" he asked. "No bags?"

"No bags," Liam confirmed. During his seven years in Doctors Without Borders, he'd learned to travel light. He'd enjoyed the job, loved the travel and seeing parts of the world hardly anyone did, and the people he'd met and helped.

But it was time to settle down. He couldn't keep flitting all over the world. His body ached and his mind wanted someplace to call home. Not Jackson Hole, but somewhere in his native Wyoming where he could enjoy nature, a slower pace of life, and maybe find someone to share his life with.

Maybe someone like Rose, whose last name he didn't know.

He followed the driver toward the sliding glass doors and turned back when he reached them. He wasn't sure why, but he didn't want to leave without seeing her again. Maybe he should've just given her his phone number. Said, "If you want to get together sometime, text me."

But such a move felt a little desperate, and even if Liam felt that way, he didn't want to come across like that.

The energy increased, and the blonde woman now dozens of feet away pointed toward the escalators. Liam followed her finger and found Rose coming down, her black bag with the flower on it at her side.

She really was stunning, and Liam couldn't move even if he wanted to. Her blonde hair the color of wheat in a variety of ripeness hung halfway down her back in loose waves and curls, and she smiled at the obvious family there to greet her.

Liam took a step back inside the airport, utterly transfixed by her. She had blue eyes—not quite as vibrant as his, but captivating nonetheless. She stepped off the escalator and the other blonde woman rushed forward to hug her.

They smiled and talked, and then Rose hugged the cowboy too. He put his hand back in her sister's, so Liam knew he wasn't with Rose. The crowd of people edged forward, and Rose cast them a glance.

She looked at her sister again, and then they turned toward the people. With her back to him, Liam couldn't quite tell what was going on. He edged to the side, trying to get a better angle without being quite so stalkerish. But those people had been. They'd been hovering like vultures.

He saw Rose and her sister signing things, like they were celebrities. Which, of course, they were. Obviously. That crowd knew them, and had waited for them.

"Sir?" the driver asked, jolting Liam out of his espionage. "Did you need something?"

Oh, he did. Rose's phone number. Where she was staying. How long she'd be in town. He needed to see her again soon, and find out everything about her.

"No," he said. But he didn't move.

Rose lifted her eyes and they landed on Liam. He knew the

moment she recognized him. Time stalled for that moment. Then she smiled, tucked her hair behind her ear, and ducked her head to talk to the woman in front of her.

She handed something back to her, and looked at Liam again, this time lifting her hand in a general wave.

He'd been caught. Heat rushed through his body, but he managed to wave back. Then he wrenched his gaze from her and strode out of the airport and into the frigid January weather.

———

"LIAM'S HERE," HIS MOM CALLED WHEN HE STEPPED THROUGH THE front door of their house. "Oh, Liam." She was already crying by the time she wrapped her arms around him. He hugged her tight, inhaling the powdery scent of her skin and the freshly laundered scent of her blouse.

"Hey, Mom."

His dad entered the foyer, which stretched for forty feet above their heads, a wide smile on his face. "Liam." He waited his turn to hug Liam, and by then, Lars had come in also. It was a regular Murphy family reunion, with everyone there.

His brother was a decade younger than him, but somehow Liam and Lars got along great. He worked in their father's real estate office, set to inherit that business when their dad retired.

After all the hugging and sniffling and smiling, Liam looked at his parents. They had gray hair he didn't remember, but they were still the same. Proper all the time, even while relaxing on a Saturday afternoon. His father wore black slacks and a white short-sleeved shirt as if he'd show houses later that day.

No tie, and the buttons didn't go all the way to his throat. But still. Who wore slacks and a dress shirt around the house? Apparently his dad—and Lars, whose shirt was a pale blue instead of white. But he could've thrown on a tie and a jacket and been the best dressed man at any event.

His mother wore a denim skirt and a blouse as she ushered

him into the kitchen for something to eat. "Are we going somewhere later?" he asked.

"No," she said, pulling out a bowl of what looked like pasta salad. "Why?"

"You guys are all dressed up." He was obviously the slacker, wearing only a polo and a pair of Dockers. Heck, even his shoes weren't up to par for hanging around the house.

"Oh, we had lunch with the Stout's," she said, as if that explained everything. When she caught him looking at her like, *And?*, she added, "They own a ton of land on the east side of town. It was a business lunch."

"Oh, a business lunch. Got it." Liam thought of his last business lunch. They'd had sandwiches from a box that a company had donated, eaten under a tent in a remote village in Nigeria, and gone over who needed the medicine they'd brought the most. There wasn't enough for everyone, so lists had been made. Those who were the most susceptible to the meningitis and malaria outbreaks would be vaccinated first.

As it turned out, there had been enough for everyone, due to Director Bisset's string-pulling to get another shipment sent.

Liam still couldn't believe that had been his last assignment. He'd returned to Geneva for a few weeks while he made sure he was disease-free and all his documents and tickets were ready for him to return to the US.

He'd miss his work with Doctors Without Borders, that was for sure. But he had new adventures to look forward to.

"So, do you have the keys to the summer cabin?" he asked.

"On the hook there." His mom nodded toward the row of hooks by the fridge. "When are you going?"

"Oh, I don't know." He sighed as he sat at the bar and let her put a plate of food in front of him. He marveled at how much they had. The opulence of where they lived and how they just opened the fridge and pulled out anything they wanted.

"It'll be difficult to get there," she said. "Coral Canyon's had a lot of snow this winter."

"Worse than here?" he asked, picking up a few noodles with his fork.

"That's what I've heard." She smiled at him. "It'll be so good for that town to have an emergency clinic."

"Hmm." Liam didn't want to talk about the clinic. It wasn't set to open until summer, and he had a ton of details to work out first. Thus, why he was moving into his parents' summer cabin when it wasn't summer.

And it wasn't a cabin either, Liam knew. It was easily as big as the mansion where he now sat eating pasta salad, and the only reason it could even be labeled a cabin was because it sat in the mountains and had a lot of wood inside. Wood floors. Wood paneling on the walls. Even a wooden countertop in the second kitchen on the bottom floor.

Liam shook his head as he thought about the place. Who needed two kitchens in a house they only stayed in for a month out of the year? It seemed ridiculous compared to some of the housing he'd seen in Columbia, Nigeria, and Chad.

It *was* ridiculous.

"So tell us about your latest assignment," his dad said, sitting next to him.

Liam didn't want to talk about that either, but it was infinitely better than them gushing about how charitable he was being by opening an emergency clinic in Coral Canyon, the town where he'd spent summers growing up.

The truth was, Liam wasn't being charitable. Sure, on the outside, it looked like he was. He'd contacted the hospital administrator and asked about space for a non-profit emergency clinic that would relieve the busyness and overcrowding in the emergency room there.

Pearl Wiley had been grateful, but skeptical. When he'd assured her he'd cover all the costs, all he needed was space, she'd still taken a couple of months to come around. But the fact was, Coral Canyon was growing and the current hospital was too small for the more robust community.

Liam wanted to help that, if he could. So maybe he was being charitable.

But no, he wasn't. He needed a fresh start, somewhere to call home, and a bit of anonymity from the Murphy name that was plastered all over Jackson Hole. And he'd loved Coral Canyon as a kid, and it felt natural to be going back there.

All he needed now was a truck to get through the snow, some clothes and shoes and winter gear, and the keys to the cabin.

Oh, and to detail his latest assignment in Nigeria. He glanced at his father, who was still waiting for him to talk. "It was great, Dad," he said, deciding to go with the lighthearted version of his job he'd been giving them for a decade. "Really great."

CHAPTER 3

Rose arranged the last of the diapers on the changing table and stepped back to survey her work. The nursery was complete. Ready for when Charlie would be able to come home from the hospital.

Everything in Rose hurt. Her muscles, from all the work putting together the crib, shopping for the dresser and changing table, hanging curtains, and setting up the rocking chair. But when tiny Charlie came home, he was going to have the best room in the whole lodge.

Lily had been home for three days now, and she was recovering as well as could be expected for a caesarian section. Her blood pressure had spiked again, and the baby was in distress. Instead of medicating her, the doctors had decided to deliver the baby as quickly as possible.

And so, five days ago, Charlie was born eight weeks early and weighed only three pounds and four ounces. He was still in the neonatal intensive care unit, and Lily and Beau spent almost all day there with him.

Lily cried every time she had to leave him there in the care of the nurses, and Rose had taken to curling up with her in bed until she quieted. Then Beau would come in, and Rose would tiptoe upstairs to her room in the lodge and shed her own tears.

Their mother was coming in a couple of days, and Vi had brought chocolate and pastries every day. Celia, the chef employed at the lodge, had made more food than an entire army could eat in a week, and Rose was so glad her sister had the love and support she needed.

And now the nursery was done too.

She turned, her thoughts also rotating to someone else. Liam.

He'd seen her signing autographs in the airport, and she wondered if he'd looked her up online. No, she wasn't Lily, out front with the microphone in her hand. But Rose was easily identifiable if someone went looking. She was in tons of pictures with Lily and Vi, and they'd even done two album covers with the three of them as the jacket.

She hummed to herself as she went down the hall past the office and into the kitchen. Whiskey Mountain Lodge was beautiful, and Rose knew why Lily had fallen in love with this place, this town, and Beau.

Coral Canyon possessed a sort of magic Rose hadn't known existed. It was peaceful. Small, but growing. Beautiful, with the Grand Teton Mountain Range hovering over it, with lakes and fields and hills and mountains.

Rose normally detested the snow, but she even found that had quite a different kind of beauty she hadn't been expecting.

In the kitchen, she poured herself a cup of coffee and moved into the dining room to look out the windows. Everything was either white with snow, or brown with mud, bark, or pathway. There was something about the contrast that spoke to the songwriter in Rose, and she thought about someone who was so black and white that they couldn't see the colors in the world.

Colors in the world. That would be a great song title. Maybe even the album title.

Rose let her thoughts rotate around, going wherever they

wanted. She knew she wouldn't be writing and recording anything with the Everett Sisters for a while.

Vi was in a serious relationship with Todd Christopherson, and while she didn't wear a ring yet, Rose expected she would be soon. And with Lily and baby Charlie…there would definitely be no songwriting in the near future.

Sadness pulled through Rose. Her entire life had been the Everett Sisters, as she was the youngest when their first album hit shelves. Only twelve. And it had been her whole life since.

She turned away from the wintry landscape and swiped her keys from the counter. Lily and Beau had already gone to the hospital that morning, and Rose said she'd be along once she finished the nursery.

She couldn't stand the thought of waiting at the window for something to happen to her. So while she didn't think hanging around the hospital sounded all that fun, it was better than being alone and wishing she knew who she was or what she wanted now that her sisters had moved on from their country music careers.

It's happening again, Rose thought as she got behind the wheel of the SUV she'd rented. She was the last to realize she even needed to move on, and the last to figure out what to do with her life now.

At the hospital, Rose basked in the busyness of it. The population in Coral Canyon had outgrown the hospital, and it had a vibrancy that didn't usually accompany a place where people came when they were sick or hurt or worse.

She looked at a sign announcing the phases of construction the hospital would undergo over the next few years as it expanded to meet the needs of a growing community. A new emergency clinic was opening in a few months to alleviate some of the traffic in the emergency room, and she liked the thought of that.

It was amazing how people had the ideas and the resources to make things better for other people. How they banded together—the way several people had around Lily and Beau during this hard time of their lives.

Rose peered closer at the sign, noticing there was a website she could visit to donate to the new clinic. A warm feeling came over her, and she pulled out her phone to type in the website. She could certainly afford to donate to a good cause.

"The new hospital is going to be nice, don't you think?"

That voice… Rose turned, but it seemed to happen in slow motion. And then she was looking into those gorgeous, ocean-colored eyes.

"Liam?"

He smiled and edged closer to her as a couple tried to get past them. Maybe he was the warm feeling she'd felt. She shoved her phone back in her coat pocket.

"Good to see you again, Rose."

Oh, he couldn't say her name like that. Now she was all tingly too.

"What are you doing here?" she asked.

"I could ask you that, too."

"I told you my sister was going to have a baby." She hooked her thumb over her shoulder. "The blood pressure medication only worked for a bit, and she delivered the baby a few days ago. He's still here, in the NICU."

She looked at him, trying to memorize all the perfectly symmetrical lines of his face. She had the strangest urge to reach up and run her fingers down his smooth jaw, trace her thumb across his lips.

Everything in her tightened, and she took a step away. *He's one of* those *people*, she reminded herself. And yet, she couldn't move much farther than a few inches.

"The baby's doing okay?" he asked.

"Well enough," Rose said.

"And your sister?"

"She's at home now. Well, she spends all her time here, but yes. She's fine."

He nodded like he really cared. "That's great."

It was then that she noticed he wore the white lab coat of a doctor. "Do you work here?"

"Sort of," he said.

"Sort of?" she repeated, her voice pitching up. "How does one sort of work at the hospital?" Feeling flirty and like she was about to step onto very thin ice, she flipped the collar on his coat. "You look like a doctor."

"I am a doctor."

Oh, be still her heart. In fact, it sort of did stall for a moment. Rose had dated exactly one doctor in her life, and he'd been handsome and charming and rich. Probably everything Liam was. But things hadn't worked out between them, mostly due to scheduling issues. And the fact that he was fifteen years older than her. Her parents definitely hadn't liked that.

But Liam couldn't be that much older than her.

"In fact," he continued. "That's my clinic. Or it will be. I'm opening it in May."

"That's your clinic?"

He grinned at the sign as if it were his child and he was proud of it. "Yep. Just here for a meeting, and I got called into a consultation. That's why I'm wearing the coat." He stuck his hands in his pockets and rocked back on his heels. "I'll admit, I didn't think I'd see you again."

Rose was still reeling from the fact that he lived here in Coral Canyon. What were the odds of that? Was this a coincidence? Or had God put them together on the plane—and again in Coral Canyon?

"So do you live here?" she blurted, her brain just now registering that he'd said he didn't think he'd see her again.

"Sort of," he answered with a devilish grin.

She couldn't help laughing, and when he joined in, her heartbeat went frantic. "Oh, I can see you're going to be a real barrel of fun."

"Well, my parents own a summer cabin here." He made

finger quotes around the words *summer cabin*. "I'm staying there while I work on getting the clinic open. Then I'll probably move into town once all the snow melts. Moving in the winter is a bear, you know?"

"I think driving in the snow would be worse," she said. He moved away from the sign, and she went with him, a quiet, slow stroll through the hospital. It didn't sound romantic. Rose had never done it with a man. But now that she was, the situation felt charged and heated in the best way. "Surely a summer cabin is in the mountains."

"That it is."

"I drive down from the mountains everyday. It's a bit on the scary side."

He looked at her, and every cell in her body burned. She'd felt this gaze on her in the airport too. It had been so strong, she'd looked up to find the person making her body buzz. And it had been Liam.

"I have a big SUV," he said. "Fresh off the lot in Jackson Hole."

"Are you from Jackson Hole?"

"I sure am. My parents and brother still live there." They turned the corner and the cafeteria doors loomed ahead. "Do you want a piece of pie?"

"Pie?" she echoed. "It's ten o'clock in the morning."

"Is that a problem? It's always a good time for pie."

Rose had a feeling she'd go anywhere and do anything to spend a bit more time with this intriguing man, so she shrugged and said, "Only if there's chocolate."

"Oh, Rose," he said with a chuckle. "This is a hospital. There's always chocolate."

CHAPTER 4

"I really can't stay long," Rose said. "I need to go see my nephew and spell my sister."

"Fifteen minutes," Liam said, desperate to keep her with him for a few more minutes. Long enough to learn her last name and get her phone number. "Do you have fifteen minutes?"

"I suppose," Rose said.

He held open the door for her, and they entered the cafeteria. "So," he said. "What's your last name?"

She cut him a glance. "You're telling me you didn't look me up? Do a search online?"

"I didn't." He'd wanted to. Plenty of times. But something always stole his attention, and when he'd come back to the thought, he'd push it away. He didn't want to learn about her online. She herself was much more fascinating.

"Everett," she said. "I'm Rose Everett." She delivered the name like it should mean something to him. Like he should recognize it. But he didn't.

"Murphy," he said. "I'm Liam Murphy."

Her eyes widened for a moment, then she relaxed. "Like the Murphy on all the signs in Jackson?"

"All my dad's real estate company," he said. "And my mom's a Hughes."

"Like the hotels?"

"That's right." He picked up a tray and moved over to the pie counter. "See? I told you they'd have chocolate."

She didn't act weird about his family name. Didn't gush about how much money he must have. He'd already mentioned the summer cabin, and she hadn't batted an eyelash at that.

She reached for a plate with the chocolate cream pie, and he noticed her nails were blue today. "New nails already?"

"I got them done for Charlie." She set the pie on his tray and looked at her hand. "He's the sweetest baby. Gets more personality every day."

Liam sure liked the softness in Rose's voice. "Do you have any kids?"

She blinked at him, and he busied himself with getting a piece of lemon meringue pie and a piece of cherry.

She laughed, a light, high sound that wasn't really made of happiness. "No," she said. "I don't have kids. Never been married. Not dating anyone."

Their eyes met, and so many things were said in those few moments. Sparks practically manifested in the air between them, and Liam wasn't so far removed from his hormones and his love life—or lack thereof—that he couldn't recognize attraction when he felt it.

"Same," he said. "On all counts."

A smile tugged at her lips, and Liam's attention dropped there for a moment. He felt like he might combust at any moment, so he turned away from the pie and asked, "Milk? Do we need milk to go with our pie?" His voice was only slightly screechy, and he covered it with a cough.

"No milk," she said. "I'm not exactly lactose intolerant, but it doesn't agree with me too well."

"I'm sure the chocolate pie has milk in it."

"It's worth the risk." She flashed him a smile and picked up a bottle of water. He chose lemonade, and they moved to the line to pay. He gave the girl a twenty, got his change, and steered them to a table in the corner.

He wasn't sure if this was a date or not, but he didn't care. He was with Rose, a woman he'd been thinking about for seven straight days and never thought he'd see again.

"So who's your sister?" he asked.

"Lily Whittaker?" she said as if she wasn't sure. "Do you know the Whittakers?"

"Sure," he said. "I mean, we're not like best buds or anything. I think the youngest is close to my age." He leaned forward as if he was going to tell her a secret. "I only spent summers in Coral Canyon."

"Beau is the youngest," she said. "He's Lily's husband." Rose took her pie and picked up a fork.

"Right, Beau." Liam didn't know him well, but he could probably pick the Whittakers out of a line-up. "And that was another sister at the airport with you?"

"Yes, Violet." She watched him again. For what, he wasn't sure.

"I gotta say," he said, digging into his cherry pie. "It looked like you were signing something there. People waiting for you. All that kind of stuff." He looked at her, his bite of pie perfectly poised for consumption. "You must be famous or something."

She watched him slide the bite of cherries and crust into his mouth. "Or something," she said, dropping her gaze to her chocolate concoction.

"What do you do?"

"I'm a country music artist," she said. "The Everett Sisters?" She met his eye, and when he didn't exclaim he knew them, she added, "We have eight albums. All platinum. I guess you could say we're famous." She shrugged again, and then took off her winter coat to reveal a pretty blue sweater.

"I feel like I should explain," he said. "I've lived overseas for ten years. Before that I was in medical school. And I don't listen to a lot of country music."

"Shocking," she said. "You grew up in Wyoming and aren't a die-hard country music fan?" The teasing quality of her voice sent shivers through Liam's muscles.

He chuckled with her and took another bite of pie.

"What were you doing overseas?" she asked. "We've been to Australia, but not many other places. Those Aussies, they like their country music."

"I bet they do." He took a deep breath. "I mostly worked in Africa, and a bit in South America, for the Doctors Without Borders program."

"Ah," she said, nodding. "That's why you can speak Spanish and Swahili. And what was the other one?"

"Portuguese," they said together.

Their eyes met again, and if Liam hadn't recognized the current between them earlier, he wouldn't be able to deny it now.

"There you are, Doctor Murphy."

The moment broke with the intrusion of Veronica Tally. A tall brunette, she was the Director of Community Events in Coral Canyon. Liam had also been avoiding her calls and texts for three straight days now.

He sighed. "Hello, Veronica." He indicated Rose. "Have you met Rose Everett?"

Veronica flicked her eyes at Rose and looked back at Liam. "Nice to—" She swung her focus back to Rose. "Rose Everett?" Her dark eyes widened and surprise emanated from her. "All the Everett Sisters are in town? Oh, you three need to do a concert!" She pulled out the chair beside Rose and flopped into it. "You really do. I've asked Vi about it so many times." Her excitement made Liam grin, because for once it wasn't directed at him.

"I see now that I didn't give you the proper reaction when you told me who you were," he said.

Rose shook her head, her lips pressed together into a straight line. She turned to Veronica, and wow, the woman could exude charm when she had to. Her voice was pleasant and firm when she said, "I'm so sorry, Veronica. Lily just had her baby, and he's here in the NICU. So we can't do a concert right now."

Veronica's face fell, but she rebounded quickly. "Maybe for Christmas!"

"Well, I don't know if I'll be around at Christmas." Rose gave Liam a look, but he couldn't tell if it was something like *Save me,* or *What do you think of me not being here at Christmas?*

He started praying she would be, that was what he thought. He'd spent a lot of time on his knees while he worked in difficult and dire circumstances in Africa, and while this certainly wasn't as devastating as dealing with someone who had the Ebola virus, he felt like if Rose left town, she'd take all the oxygen with her.

"We should still—"

"Did you need me, Veronica?" Liam asked, interrupting her and throwing his napkin on top of his second piece of pie. "Because I'm afraid I have to get going." He stood as if he'd leave right now, without Rose's phone number.

"Yes," she said, standing and regaining her professional demeanor. "It's about the Valentine's Day bachelor auction, as I've texted you several times."

Liam waited, already knowing what she was going to ask him.

"We need you, Doctor Murphy. You'd be a huge draw, being new in town and so handsome...." She let her words hang there as she ran her gaze down to his toes and back. She cleared her throat. "All the money goes to community programs for the youth, and some is even going to the hospital fund."

Liam looked at Rose, who watched him with delight in her eyes and a smile on her face. Would she bid on him if he did the auction? Would she even be in town come Valentine's Day?

"When is the auction?" she asked.

"We do it on February twelfth," Veronica said. "That way, all the single women have a date on Valentine's Day. They're happy.

We've raised money. The bachelor auction helps *a lot* of people." She had a distinct pleading note in her voice. "*Please*, Doctor Murphy."

Rose giggled and said, "She said please."

He couldn't ask her if she'd be there. But if she was…Liam wanted to be too. "Fine," he said with a sigh, like he'd just committed to having his hands cut off. "I'll do it."

Veronica squealed and clapped her hands. "Great. I'll send you the forms we need you to sign. Then you just show up." She grinned at both of them and clicked away in her high heels.

Liam looked at Rose again. He wanted to ask her on a real date, not a walk to get hospital pie from the cafeteria. He wanted to ask her if she'd be at the bachelor auction. He wanted her phone number.

"So," he said, deciding to go for the easiest option, the one that could get him the other two. "What are the chances I can get your phone number?"

She held out her palm and said, "Give me your phone."

He complied, the brief moment where his fingers touched hers causing a riot inside his chest. She swiped and tapped and handed his device back. "There you go." She picked up the pace now. "Thanks for the pie, Doctor Murphy. See you later."

He paused and let her go ahead of him, watching until she rounded the corner. Then he opened his phone to see if she'd really put in her number. She had, and a smile as wide as the River Niger crossed his face.

Everything about being in Coral Canyon had just gotten better, and Liam's prompting to come back to this town where he hadn't been in twenty years felt confirmed.

"Thank you, Lord," he whispered to the empty hallway. Leaving Doctors Without Borders had been very difficult for him. Coming home had too.

But maybe the Lord had a reason for pushing Liam in that direction, and the reason was Rose Everett.

CHAPTER 5

"Day seventeen," Rose said to Lily. She sat at the kitchen counter in the lodge, already ready to go down to the hospital. Her sister looked tired, and she wasn't dressed yet. She wore a baggy purple robe over her pajama pants and her hair seemed like it hadn't been washed in a few days.

Rose couldn't even imagine how hard it was for Lily to leave Charlie every night.

"Yeah." She sighed as she poured herself a cup of coffee. "It's killing me we can't bring him home yet."

"We will soon," Beau said as he entered the kitchen behind her.

Lily looked like she might cry, but she nodded, sipped her coffee, and set it on the counter. "I'm going to go shower. Then we can go." She left Rose alone with Beau in the kitchen.

"What are we going to do for her?" Rose asked, this sense of helplessness inside her almost too painful. Too deep. She felt like she was drowning, and Charlie wasn't even her baby.

"She's doing okay," Beau said.

"Beau," Rose said, putting on her bossy voice. "She is *not* okay."

"Charlie is doing so much better," Beau said, almost a note of panic in his voice. "He's pinking up, and he's almost off the oxygen. He's gaining weight." He turned from the coffee maker, but he hadn't even gotten down a mug from the cupboard. "I can *feel* it. He's going to come home soon."

Rose realized this was really hard for Beau too. He'd just been better at hiding it. "We still need to do something."

"Like what, Rose?"

Rose told herself he didn't mean to snap at her. That she had no idea what her sister and brother-in-law were going through. "I think I should take her this afternoon. Go get our nails done or go to a movie. Get out of the hospital for a little bit."

"She won't go."

Rose slid off the barstool. "I'll talk to her."

Beau frowned as Rose marched out of the kitchen, and she knew he didn't like the way Lily sometimes relied on her and Vi. But at this point, she didn't care. She, Vi, and Lily had been through so much as sisters, and singers, and all of it.

She rapped lightly on Lily's bedroom door, which was right across from the nursery that still hadn't been used. "Lils?" she said as she entered. "It's just me, Rose."

From the bathroom, Lily said, "I'm not dressed, Rose."

"Okay." She closed the door behind her and pressed her back into it. "Look, we need to go do something this afternoon. Just me, and you, and Vi." She hadn't talked to Vi yet, but she didn't have a job—unless training her boyfriend's dog counted, and Rose didn't think it did. Vi could spare a few hours.

She pulled out her phone as she continued to talk. "I'm thinking nails. Or a massage. Or a movie."

"I can't get a massage," Lily said, her voice carrying a heaviness Rose didn't like. "I can't lie on my stomach, and I can't get on and off the table." The water started to run in the sink, and Rose sent a quick text to Vi about her availability that afternoon.

"A movie then," Rose called. "You love the movie theater popcorn."

"I don't want to leave Charlie." The water turned off, and

Rose realized she was facing a bigger hill than she'd originally thought.

"Vi's in," Rose said as she read Vi's response. She took a few steps toward the bathroom. "Lils, it's really not healthy for you to spend all day and all evening over there. It's just a few hours. Beau will be there. He said he'd take care of Charlie."

Rose had seen them both holding their son, pulling back their collars so Charlie could be skin-to-skin with them, so they could bond. Rose had felt the love revolving around them, and she wanted it for herself.

Liam's handsome face filled her mind, but she pushed against him. She needed to focus on her sister, not her could-be boyfriend who'd only texted her a handful of times. He hadn't asked her out yet, and he'd never once asked if she'd be at the Valentine's Day bachelor auction.

But Rose had it on her calendar, and she was planning on being there. She wasn't sure what kind of money the other single women in town were willing to spend on a gorgeous doctor, but Rose was betting she could out-bid them.

She hoped she could, because if Liam wasn't going to ask her out, she'd win his date in the auction and then he'd have no choice but to go out with her.

If only February twelfth wasn't still eleven days away.

Lily appeared in the bathroom doorway, dressed and her hair damp. "Okay, Rose," she said. "A couple of hours at the theater. And you're buying the popcorn." She flashed a smile, but it wasn't anywhere near as brilliant as Rose knew Lily could do.

"Deal," she said, moving forward to wrap her sister in a hug. "He's going to come home soon, sis."

"Let's go find out," Lily said, combing her fingers through her hair and gathering it all into a ponytail.

Rose's phone went off again, and both she and Lily looked at it. "Who's Liam Murphy?" Lily asked.

"No one," Rose said quickly, shoving her phone in her back

pocket. The need to read his message burned through her, but she didn't have a way to know what he was. Yet.

"Rose," Lily said in a warning voice, her face brightening. "Do you have a secret boyfriend?"

"What?" She scoffed. "No, of course not."

"Knock, knock," Beau said, and Lily rounded toward him.

"Do you know a Liam Murphy?" She tossed Rose a playful glare, and this was more like the Lily that she knew.

"Liam Murphy?" Beau repeated. "I—that name is a bit familiar, but I'm not sure I know him."

Rose threw Lily a triumphant smile. "And he knows everyone in town."

"Wait. Isn't he the doctor doing that emergency clinic?"

"Ooh, a doctor. Did you meet him at the hospital?" Lily asked in a singsong voice.

"No," Rose said flatly. "He was actually on my flight here a couple of weeks ago."

"*And* he's opening the clinic here?" Lily's teasing faded into pure glee. "It's fate!"

"It's not fate," Rose said, rolling her eyes and stepped toward Lily and Beau. "Come on. Charlie needs us."

Rose drove herself down the canyon, because she didn't stay as long as Lily and Beau, and she liked having a car to go grab food or just to get away. How her sister had stayed so long each day spoke of her love and dedication to her newborn son.

So she didn't allow herself to read Liam's message until she'd parked at the hospital. *Sorry I've been so busy. Wondering if you'd like to grab dinner sometime?*

He'd texted again a moment later. *Or lunch.*

Or breakfast.

Or coffee.

Or pie.

Basically, I want to eat and I want to do it with you.

By the end of his text string, Rose was laughing. "Finally," she whispered as she tapped out her response.

I eat. And I could see you again. You seem busier than me. Tell me when, and I'll consult my schedule.

She wondered if it was a mistake to get involved with Liam. After all, he was making a life and career for himself here in Coral Canyon, and while Rose didn't have plans to leave town anytime soon, she did *not* live here.

And the last doctor she'd dated never had time for her either. He was always too busy. And this doctor was opening a brand new clinic and could barely text her.

"Maybe he just doesn't like texting," she told herself as she turned off the vehicle and prepared to enter the freezing temperatures outside. As she hurried through the chilly morning to the entrance she'd seen Lily and Beau go through a few minutes ago, she listed all the things about Liam she knew.

He liked to talk to people on the plane. He was smart. Dashing. Charming. Busy. Didn't get ruffled by confrontation. Enjoyed cherry pie—and that was a black mark against him. Rose didn't think fruit should be forced into pies, but she'd managed to keep her opinion to herself during their pie binge a couple of weeks ago.

She half-expected to run into Liam on her way up to the NICU, but she didn't. Lily had Charlie cuddled against her chest, humming to him as she rocked him. He really was the most beautiful baby. He was pink, and he had the most beautiful blond hair that wisped around his head.

Rose ran her fingers lightly along his head and grinned down at her sister. "Liam finally asked me out."

Lily smiled back and paused her melody. "So he *is* your secret boyfriend."

"I mean, not really." Rose sighed happily. "But he's in the Valentine's Day auction, and I'm going to win him."

"Oh, boy," Lily said. "Listen to yourself, Rose. He's not a prize."

"I know that."

"But sometimes you forget," Lily said. "I have to go to the

bathroom again. Beau is talking to the nurses. Can you take Charlie?"

"Of course." Rose got some time with Charlie everyday, and it really was the highlight of her time in Coral Canyon. She cradled the baby in her arms, her whole heart melting as he groaned and grunted while he settled.

Lily left and Rose took her place in the rocking chair, whispering to the baby, "Oh, you're the best boy in the world, aren't you?" She stroked his cheek and pulled down her own collar so Charlie could snuggle into her skin too. He was warm and wonderful, and Rose loved him so, so much.

She closed her eyes as she rocked, in absolute heaven with this baby in her arms.

———

"What do you mean, you have to go?" Vi hissed as Rose stood with only ten minutes left in the movie.

"She has a date," Lily said.

"I tried to get him—" Rose started, but she cut off. She hadn't tried to get a different time with Liam. He'd suggested they go that night, and it was only ten minutes of the movie she'd have to miss. Lily had been fine with it, especially after Rose had explained how busy he was, and that she'd been waiting to be asked out for almost two weeks.

Rose stumbled over her sister with a, "I'll call you later."

"Have fun," Lily said, her focus already back on the movie.

Rose made it to her truck without slipping on the ice, and her phone chimed as she started the engine. *Thanks for the movie, baby sister. It was exactly what I needed.*

She smiled at Lily's text and sent a few hearts back. Then she focused on getting across town to someplace called Devil's Tower that Liam had promised her would change her mind about stacks of things.

They were meeting, because she had told him she'd already

be in town. He hadn't asked where, and she'd suggested they meet. He'd suggested the time, and she pulled up to the restaurant with three minutes to spare.

She pulled out her lip gloss and made her lips pinky and shiny before she stepped through the lot, avoiding puddles and piles of snow, to the door.

Liam came out before she went in, and he smiled at her. "Aren't you a sight for sore eyes?" His deep voice reached all the way into her soul and made her cells vibrate. She glanced down at her black coat when he did.

"I'm wearing a coat and jeans," she said. "It is *freezing* here. Does it ever get warm?"

"Oh, sure." He ushered her inside. "About July."

"At least it's warm in here." She didn't move forward as Liam crowded in behind her. His hand bumped hers and then held on.

"It really is great to see you."

Rose twisted and smiled at him. "You too."

"They're waiting for us." He nudged her forward and he nodded to the hostess. "We're ready now."

She gave him a flirtatious smile and plucked two menus from the holder on the side of her podium. "Right this way." She didn't look at Rose at all.

Once they had a booth, and Rose had shed her coat, she asked, "How are things going at the clinic?"

"Great," he said with a sigh. "Fine." He put a smile on his face. "I don't want to talk about the clinic. How's your sister's baby?"

"Still in the NICU." Rose added a sigh to the conversation too. "My sister and I took her to a movie this afternoon to get her out of the hospital for a little bit."

"Good idea," he said. He glanced up at the waitress as she set two glasses of water on the table.

"You two know what you want?"

Liam threw her a sly, flirty look that made Rose feel like the luckiest woman in the world. "I do. Care if I order for us?"

Rose wanted nothing more. "Go right ahead."

He smiled, and he really should be locked up for looking so good while doing that. "We'll have the Ring Tower, and the Cheese Me Tower." He looked back at her. "How do you feel about fried chicken?"

"I'm from the South," she answered.

"And the Clucker Tower. Oh, and the Let's Make a Dill Tower."

Rose started laughing as the waitress continued to scribble on her pad. "Can we eat all of this?"

"Oh, sure," he said. "And the Leafy Tower. That should do it."

The waitress gave him a quick smile, said, "Coming right up," and walked away.

Rose reached for the menu before she forgot the things he'd said. "What is this place?"

He grabbed her menu before she could look at it. "It's a surprise. But everything here comes in a tower or a stack. You're going to love it."

"Is that right?" She leaned her elbows on the table and cradled her face in her hands.

"That's right." He tucked the menus down by his legs on the seat. "So, Rose Everett. I've been listening to a brand new country music trio. They're really quite talented."

Warmth pulled through Rose with the strength of gravity, and all she could do was smile.

CHAPTER 6

I'll be there.

Liam had been living on those three words for almost two weeks now. Since the very successful date at Devil's Tower —he was so glad he'd tacked on the Leafy Tower, which was basically a salad in vertical form—he'd been texting Rose every day. Every spare moment, actually.

He'd finally gotten up the courage to ask her if she'd be coming to the Valentine's Day bachelor auction, and she'd texted back *I'll be there.*

The event was that night, and Liam couldn't wait to see Rose again. They'd been out a couple more times, but he'd been rushed each time, and once they'd just met for coffee and banana bread at the coffee shop for twenty minutes before a meeting with the hospital administrator.

As he finished shaving, his phone chimed with the sound he'd set just for Rose, and he almost cut himself in his haste to look at his device. *Best news ever! Charlie is coming home tonight!*

His heart skipped and jumped for a couple of reasons. One, taking a baby home was excellent news. But two, would she skip the auction that night to spend time with her nephew at home?

He wasn't going to ask. He wasn't a jerk.

That's so great! he sent back. *Tell Lily and Beau congratulations.* Then he splashed aftershave on his face and stepped into his best suit. He knew how to dress the part like his parents did, and this time he had the right shoes and all the right pieces in the right places.

He had an obligation to do the auction, and all he could do was pray that Rose would be there. So he did that, buttoned his wool coat, and stepped into the garage to get into his LandRover.

The auction was being held at the community center, and by the time Liam pulled up—twenty minutes early, when he was appointed to arrive—the parking lot was already full.

Full.

He heard the chattering of female voices as he entered, but Veronica swept him down a hall quickly, saying, "Okay, you're here. Good. Everyone's here."

"I'm last?" he asked.

"I staggered the arrival times," she said, almost shoving him into a room with a couple dozen other men. "Julia will help you with your number." The door slammed closed, and Liam straightened his tie and glanced around, trying to regain his composure.

An auburn-haired woman sat at a table nearby, and she held out a crisp square of paper with the number nine on it. "Hello, Doctor Murphy. You'll be number nine, and I'll let you know when it's your turn to go backstage."

He took his number and stared at it. "I wear this?"

"Yep," Julia said. "Pin it where you'd like." She handed him a safety pin, and Liam moved away from the table. Some of the men stood together in groups, talking. But the majority of them sat in chairs facing a big-screen television. It showed the stage in the event room, and chatter could be heard but no women could be seen.

"How many women are there?" he asked the man he sat beside, still trying to figure out where to pin his number.

His phone vibrated in his pocket as the guy said, "At least fifty."

"There's not fifty of us," Liam said.

"Nope."

So not every single woman in Coral Canyon would have a date on Valentine's Day. He pulled his phone out and looked at it. Rose had texted again. *I'm running late. Will I miss you?*

There were fifteen minutes before it started and he was number nine. He had no idea how long the auction would take. *I'm number nine,* he said. *And I have no idea how fast it goes.*

At least now he knew Rose intended to bid on him. And he'd done a little digging on her since seeing Veronica's reaction in the hospital cafeteria a few weeks ago. It had only taken a little, because the Everett Sisters were huge. *Huge* country music artists.

Which meant Rose had plenty of money and could likely outbid any woman currently in the event room.

I'll hurry.

Liam tucked his phone away and decided to pin his number on his lapel like it was a boutonniere. Then he faced the television and wished his stomach didn't feel like it had been filled with jumping beans.

Finally, Veronica appeared on the stage and took the mic. "Are we ready for the auction, ladies?"

Whoops and cheers went up, and Veronica smiled widely. "Remember, all proceeds go to fund the youth programs here at the Community Center in Coral Canyon. A percentage of our proceeds this year are also being donated to the hospital, to help with the renovation and remodel. So it's a good cause, ladies! Pull out those wallets!"

Twittering came through the TV, and the excitement from the other room seemed to infect Liam too. He wasn't a huge fan of the bachelor auction, but it did bring in money for the town, and a lot of women would have dates on one of the hardest days of the year for singles, and he'd heard of a few couples who'd made a love connection and had gone on to get married after meeting through the auction.

Liam directed his thoughts away from marriage. He'd been out with Rose a few times. He wanted to see her every day, but he had a clinic to get open and it wasn't as easy as he'd anticipated to get the staff he needed. And the red tape from the hospital? Unbelievable.

The first man was taken out by Julia, and she returned to get Bachelor Number Two while Veronica read Number One's resume. Liam's stomach squirmed. He'd provided his own bio, but it was only a couple of sentences long. He wasn't sure what it would be used for, and had he known, he would've beefed it up a bit, the way Number One obviously had.

Doesn't matter, he told himself. Rose was coming.

But what if Rose didn't make it? What if no one bid on him? And he just stood up there like a loser, wishing he didn't have to be the one to solve the problem. The one to score the highest on his latest exam. The one dressed perfectly, so his parents would be proud of him.

He shook his head and breathed. He wasn't in high school anymore. Had given up the family business. Graduated at the top of his class in medical school. Worked in remote locations with little more than masking tape and gauze.

And even if Rose didn't show up, he hoped someone would still bid on him. He was wearing his best suit, after all.

One by one, the men were taken out, and it was finally his turn. He stood off-stage while Number Eight brought in quite a lot of bids. There seemed to be a war going on for him, and Liam wished he'd paid attention during his introduction.

He was finally won with a bid of five hundred and twelve dollars, and he was taken off the other side of the stage.

Liam slicked his palms down his thighs and waited for Veronica to look in his direction. Julia had said she wouldn't be able to see him, but he should go out when she looked to his side.

"And now," she said into the mic like she had a great secret. "We have one of Coral Canyon's newest and most eligible bachelors…." She looked at Liam, and he almost tripped over his feet as he started toward her.

"*Doctor* Liam Murphy," she said as he stepped into the lights on the stage. He squinted, as his eyes adjusted to the bright light, but he could certainly hear the whispers in the crowd.

"He needs no introduction, but he is a general practitioner who's spent the last eleven years working in places like Columbia, Chad, and Nigeria in his work for Doctors Without Borders. He's back in town, where he spent his childhood summers, to open the new emergency clinic this May."

She looked at her notes like there would be more, and when she didn't find it, she faced the crowd again. Liam was suddenly glad the lights were so bright so he couldn't see the faces out there.

He hoped and prayed Rose was out there.

"So let's start the bidding, shall we?" Veronica said brightly, something she was very good at. "Do I have fifty dollars?"

To Liam's great relief, a female voice said, "Fifty dollars!"

He stood there, smiling, while Veronica managed the bids. He hadn't heard Rose's voice yet, and he was starting to wonder if he would recognize it even if she was there—which he had no guarantee of.

"Could he be our largest bid of the evening?" Veronica practically yelled into the microphone. "Do I hear five-fifteen?"

A long silence came, and Liam wasn't sure why he cared if he was the highest bid of the night or not. Besides, there were still a lot of men to go, and any one of them could fetch more money.

"One thousand dollars," a voice came from the back of the room.

A collective gasp rose up, and then Rose added, "Is that not enough? *Two* thousand dollars."

Liam couldn't help it. He started laughing.

CHAPTER 7

Rose stood at the payment table, listening to a woman named Julia gush about her high bid. Foolishness raced through Rose. She'd arrived to find Liam standing on the stage, and silence surrounding him. She hadn't known where the bid was, and she hadn't wanted to lose him.

She hadn't had time to ask anyone.

So she'd shouted out a thousand dollars. Why everyone had frozen after that, she hadn't been sure. She knew now, but she was still writing a check for two thousand dollars. The money didn't concern her, but the perception of the rest of the women in the event room did.

And Liam….

She almost groaned out loud. Ripping off her check, she handed it to Julia, said, "Thank you," and held her head high as she walked out. Some of the other women who'd already paid for their bachelor were milling about, talking to the man they'd won.

Phone numbers were being exchanged, and Valentine's Day plans made. Rose just wanted to go back to the lodge, hold her baby nephew while she told him all about the debacle, and then crawl into bed and stay there.

She didn't need to go out on Valentine's Day. Mother Nature was supposed to dump inches of snow that day anyway.

"Rose," Liam said from somewhere behind her, and her step stuttered. She'd have to face him sometime, but it didn't have to be right now. She kept going toward the exit. Maybe if they had to talk, it could be in private.

In fact, most of what Rose wanted to do with Liam required privacy.

She banished the fantasies and stood in the entryway between the outside doors and the inner doors. A few moments later, Liam joined her.

"You made it," he said, taking both of her hands in his. Her mind blanked for a moment at his touch, then her cells and nerves started firing like cannons.

"Barely," she said, her voice hardly above a whisper.

He ran his hands up her arms, and though she wore a blue sweatshirt with a stag on it, her skin reacted to his touch. "I was worried there for a moment." He seemed genuinely concerned about her. "You okay? How's Charlie?"

Rose inhaled and looked up into Liam's vibrant eyes. "He's so great." She almost blurted that she wanted a dozen babies like him, but she caught the words before they left her throat. "I'm sorry about that in there," she said. "I didn't know what the bid was at, and I was just…."

She let her words die. She didn't need to admit to him that she was desperate to win him, that she didn't want anyone else to have the pleasure of going out with him.

"I know," he said, drawing her into his arms. She went willingly, because he was warm, and she was cold. Because he was strong, and she was weak. Because she liked him, and when held her close, she felt as if he liked her too.

"Have you had time to eat tonight?" he asked. "We could go grab something."

She nodded, because she'd like that.

"You have eaten?" he asked. "Or you want to go get something?"

Rose found her courage and her well of strength. "I want to go get something."

"All right," he said. "Let's go." He threaded his fingers through hers and led her outside, where the real cold air stole the breath right from her lungs.

"Wow," she said, her teeth chattering instantly. "I don't know how people live here in the winter."

"Right?" He chuckled, which alleviated some of the tension between them. "That's why we only came in the summer."

"Tell me about that," Rose said as he unlocked his LandRover and helped her up and in.

His fingers slid down her arm and he watched her for a moment before closing the door and rounding the front of the SUV. Once he was behind the wheel, he started adjusting dials and pushing buttons.

"Your seat warmer is on now," he said. "Takes a few seconds." His car heated faster than any she'd ever been in, and Rose knew better than most what a lot of money could buy.

"We came for June and July, usually," he said, backing out of the parking space. "I'm ten years older than my brother, so for a while there, it was just me and my mom. I'd leave the house in the morning with a fishing pole and a sack lunch, and I wouldn't come back until dinnertime." He laughed again and shook his head. "Life was easy."

"Is life hard now?"

"No," he said. "It's just different."

"Did your dad not come to the cabin?"

"Oh, no. Summer is the best time to sell houses," Liam said, a quiet note of unrest in his voice. "He'd come up on weekends if he wasn't busy. And once Lars came along and was old enough to walk, I'd take him to the lake, the rivers, fishing, hiking, all of it."

"Sounds nice," she said, thinking of what she did when she was twelve.

"It was nice," he said. "I do love the cabin. After a while, I realized how much money my family has." He cut her a glance, as if she hadn't figured out his parents—and him—were loaded. "And I didn't want to spend my life wearing ties and selling land and mansions. My dad didn't take it super well."

"Oh?" Not being in the family business had never been an option for Rose, so she understood.

"No. He inherited Murphy Real Estate from his father, who inherited it from his father. You know how it goes."

"I do." She looked out the window as he crawled down Main Street.

"Burgers?" he asked. "Or pizza."

"Pizza," she said. "Look, that says a pizza buffet." She swung her head toward him. "Is that really true?"

"Yeah, sure," he said, swinging into Pie Squared, which was fairly new in town. "It's pretty good too."

Rose had never eaten so well in her life. But Celia kept the fridge at the lodge stocked so well, and the mom-and-pop joints in town had all been excellent.

Liam held the door for her as they entered, and the scent of cheese and bread and marinara sauce filled the air, making Rose's stomach grumble.

"So is your brother going to take over the real estate company?" she asked.

"Yeah." Liam studied the menu, and then ended up ordering the buffet.

"Me too," Rose said, and they both got drinks too. After filling hers with orange soda, she sat in the booth and waited for him to join her. "You know, being part of the Everett Sisters was never something I chose. I couldn't not choose it either."

"I'll bet not," he said.

"I loved it though." She heard the wistful quality of her

voice. "But with Charlie, and Vi getting married, I'm not sure we'll ever make another album."

"What about making one of your own?"

Rose shook her head. "It's not the same. Vi did that a couple of years ago, and it was sort of a flop."

"What? It only sold a few hundred thousand copies instead of a million?" Liam looked at her with sparkling blue eyes, full of sarcasm and teasing.

"Yeah," she said, smiling. "Something like that."

He shook his head and smiled. "Everyone has a different definition of success, you know?"

"Oh, I know."

He got up. "Should we get some food?"

She joined him, piling her plate full of salad and then adding a second plate with pizza. When she finally got back to the table, he grinned at her and said, "Wow, look at you."

"Right?" She picked up a piece of the baked potato pizza. "I hope this is good."

"It is." He indicated that he'd gotten a piece too. "I like the barbecue chicken the best."

"Clearly." She took a bite of her pizza, noticing he had three of the barbecue chicken slices on his plate. After she chewed and swallowed, she asked, "So why'd you become a doctor?"

He set down his half-finished piece of pizza and wiped his mouth. "I've never had to want for anything. And honestly, I was a little embarrassed. So I wanted to help people. People who didn't have anything. I've always liked math and science and stuff like that, so I went to college in biology, and then onto medical school."

She nodded along. "And you got to help people."

His face turned haunted for a few moments, and he seemingly entered memories only he knew about. "Yeah," he finally said, putting a plastic smile on his face. "I helped people."

Rose cocked her head. "Why do you do that?"

"Do what?" He picked up his food again.

"Did you not like your job? Whenever you talk about it, you just gloss over things. There's no details."

He gazed at her evenly, something hot sparking in his eyes. She wasn't sure if it was more like passion or more like annoyance. Maybe both.

"The details aren't pretty," he said.

"Is that why you quit?"

"One of the reasons," he said, maybe the most honestly he ever had. "It was…difficult to see the circumstances some people live in. Of no choice of their own, but because of tyranny or war or simply not having a government that functions. Very difficult."

"You go somewhere else when you think of it," she said quietly.

"Do I?"

"Mm hm." She took a long drink of her soda while he visited his memories again. "See? You're doing it right now."

He blinked and looked down at the pizza he held in his hand. "I guess I do. I hadn't realized that."

"Which was the worst country?" she asked.

"We don't need to talk about it."

"Why not?" Rose asked. "Your work with Doctors Without Borders was a huge part of your life for a lot of years. You don't want to talk about it?"

"I really don't." His jaw clenched, and Rose decided to drop the subject.

"All right." She started mixing her salad all together to get the dressing evenly distributed. "What do you want to talk about then?"

"Tell me something about you I don't know," he said.

"Oh, I'm an open book." Rose laughed, because that wasn't really true. Sure, there was plenty to read online, but only some of it was true. "Been singing and writing songs with my sisters since I was a child. First album hit it big when I was only twelve. Still doing it now, all these years later."

"How old are you?

"Thirty-five."

"Did you like the singing and song-writing?"

"Definitely."

"Ever wanted to do something else?"

Rose paused, because she did have something, but she didn't want to admit it. She wasn't even sure she'd admitted it out loud to herself yet.

"Ah, I see it there." Liam smiled in a calm, gentle way. "Not so easy when it's you, is it?"

Rose took another bite of salad and shook her head. "I know what it is, but I'm…worried it'll scare you off."

"Scare me off?" He reached across the table and covered her hand with his. "In case you haven't noticed, Rose, I like you."

I like you.

"And I know we're just getting to know each other, but you —something is different about you."

"You haven't dated very many women, have you?" she asked, leaning back into the booth behind her.

"I mean, a few." He shrugged.

"I've been out with eight men in the past nine months," she said. "Well, ten months now that I've been here. Oh wow. Nine men in ten months." A flush of heat stained her cheeks and she took another big bite of salad so she wouldn't be able to talk for a minute or two.

"Nine men?" he asked.

She nodded.

"Like me? Like, you've been out with them more than once? Held their hand? Or are we talking first dates?"

She held up her finger while she chewed, so glad she'd given herself the extra time. She finally swallowed and said, "Like you. Kissed two of them."

Liam sat back in his seat too, as if she'd just hit him with something heavy. "Okay."

"Is that weird?" she asked, but she knew it was. "Honestly,

now that I've seen my sisters find someone to love, I want it too. So I've been actively trying to find someone."

"So I guess you know pretty early if you like a guy or not."

"I guess so."

"And you just paid two grand to go out with me."

"Yeah, that was called stupidity. I mean, look at us? I could've had it for free." She grinned at him, and he laughed, and it was the most wonderful sound in the world.

They continued eating and chatting about easier things. When he got back to the community center, where she'd left her car, he lingered near her door and said, "Don't think I didn't realize that you never told me what you wanted to do if you weren't a singer."

"Oh, I know you realized," she said. "You're much too smart to let that go."

"So you're not going to tell me?" He ran his hand up her arm and back to her fingers. Over and over again. She thought it might be natural to stretch up onto her toes and kiss him, but she wasn't quite ready for that yet.

"Not tonight." She turned and opened her car door. "Thanks for dinner."

"Thanks for bidding on me."

"So I'll see you on Valentine's Day?" She looked up at him expectantly.

"Absolutely." He leaned down and pressed his lips to her forehead.

"Good," she said when he pulled away, the sparks still shooting into her brain. "Because I paid a lot of money for that date."

He laughed, and she got in her car, and when she was all the way back to the lodge, she whispered, "A mom. I really want to be a mom of a lot of little boys and girls."

With brilliant, blazing blue eyes like Liam's.

CHAPTER 8

L iam had insisted on driving up to Whiskey Mountain Lodge for his date with Rose. He hadn't once picked her up at home to take her out, and while he wasn't purely a traditionalist, he wanted her to know he'd come to her.

But as he squinted through the snow falling rapidly against his windshield, he wondered if they should be going out tonight at all. The roads were already slick and snow-packed, and he hadn't even made it up to the lodge yet. The thought of coming down had his stomach in knots.

His phone sounded and his car said, "Message from Rose Everett."

"Read it," he told the computer, and it said, "Maybe we should cancel for tonight. It's snowing so hard. Have you left yet?"

"Call Rose Everett," he told the car next.

After a brief pause, it said, "Calling Rose Everett."

"Hey," she said a moment later, her voice anxious even through the stereo system. "I'm fine if we cancel. The wind is howling up here, and there's so much snow."

"I know," he said. "I'm driving in it. I think I'm about

halfway there." He squinted at the approaching road sign. "Two miles," he said. "I'm two miles away."

"Oh, so you're almost here."

"Don't sound so happy about it."

"I'm happy about it," she said, but she didn't sound like it. Liam wasn't sure he was happy about it either. "But I don't think we'll be leaving again. Beau said they just have everyone stay at the lodge when it snows like this. Celia's here, and so is Annie. She came to clean this morning, and decided not to drive back down."

"Yeah, I think they're smart. I don't think we'll be going down either."

"So I'll see if there's something we can eat here. And we'll put a movie on in the theater room."

It didn't sound terribly romantic—especially with four other people and a baby in the house—but Liam didn't see any other options. "Sure," he said brightly. "Sounds fun."

"You're such a liar," she said with a laugh. "I'll let you go so you can focus on the road. See you soon."

"Bye," he said, and the call disconnected. He gripped the steering wheel and flipped the LandRover into four-wheel-drive. He most certainly did not want to drive off the road tonight. Then cops and paramedics would have to come, and they shouldn't be out in these weather conditions either.

Ten long minutes later, he finally pulled into the parking lot at Whiskey Mountain Lodge. All the windows glowed with light, and it felt like a beacon of hope to him. He pulled all the way under the roof that went over the circle drive and hurried to the door.

He knocked, almost getting blown over by that wind Rose had mentioned.

"Got it!" she called, and a few seconds later, she opened the door. She wore a red dress that hugged every curve and fell to her knee. Her hair cascaded in lovely waves over her shoulders, and she looked ready for a hot Valentine's Day date—one they wouldn't be having.

Liam licked his lips and said, "Wow." He honestly had no other words for the goddess standing in front of him.

"My nails match my lipstick," she said, which were also both red.

"Amazing." He stepped into the house, glad when she didn't give him an inch. He put one arm around her waist and leaned down to inhale the scent of her hair. "You're so beautiful."

"Thank you." she stayed in his arms for another moment, and then said, "I should probably close this door."

He moved out of the way, and she did close the door, and Liam took in the grandeur and beauty of the lodge. "This place is beautiful. I think I remember hearing it burned down?"

"It did," Rose said. "A while ago. Apparently Beau's brother bought it after it was restored, and they've been living here and renting rooms since. Though, I think I heard them talking the other day that they're going to stop renting out the rooms."

She stepped down one stair into the living area and swept her hand up the steps. "Lots of rooms up there. Beau said you can have any one that Celia, Annie, or I'm not using."

His eyes followed the steps up and then down a hallway to another doorway. "You're staying up there?"

"Yes." She looked at him with curiosity. "So?"

"So are there other rooms somewhere?" he asked. "You're so tempting, and all I can think about is kissing you."

Rose's eyes widened even as a smile touched her mouth. "Is that so?"

"Did I say that out loud?" He chuckled and cleared his throat. "What I meant to say was that sure, I can pick a room up there that no one is using."

Rose giggled and shook her head. "Come on. Celia made pork chops and fried potatoes for dinner, and we have the kitchen all to ourselves for a little bit." She started through the living room, which was decorated beautifully with all the high-end textiles. "Oh, and what's with the cowboy hat?"

He followed her. "What? You don't like it?"

She turned back when she reached the doorway. "Oh, I like it." Her blue eyes glittered, and Liam thought it would be very hard not to kiss her that night. "I've just never seen you wear one."

"Well, it seemed like every man at the auction was wearing one, and I felt like maybe I couldn't be a true resident of Coral Canyon without a cowboy hat. So I bought one."

Rose shook her head as if he was some silly schoolboy. Maybe he was. "It looks great on you, I'll give you that." She moved straight through the doorway and into the kitchen. Liam saw a hall in both directions, and a mudroom to his left, but he went where Rose was.

"Smells great in here." He wrapped his arms around her from behind her and swayed, glad when she giggled and moved with him.

"Stop it," she said playfully. "We're not alone here, you know."

"Oh, believe me." He inhaled her hair again, his heart beating a rate it hadn't in a long, long time. "I know." He stepped back and moved around the counter from her, thinking it the safest place for him to behave himself.

She pulled two plates out of the oven that were already ready to be served. "Here we go."

"Who is this Celia?" he asked as his mouth started watering at the sight of the browned pork chops and crispy potatoes. "I feel like I need to get me one of her."

Rose stepped past him and put their plates on the dining room table. The lights were lower in here, and Liam thought maybe they'd get their romantic meal and date after all. And could he really kiss her later? Why couldn't he stop thinking about it?

"She's the chef here at the lodge. Works a few days a week.

She's like a member of the family." She flashed him a smile and slid into her seat. He took the one at the head of the table, only inches from her, his pulse still rioting like he'd never kissed a woman before.

He couldn't help thinking that Rose was in a different class of women, and it had been a while since he'd had any romantic feelings for someone. Maybe they were simply making up for lost time.

"So." She picked up her fork and speared a potato. "Do you go to church, Doctor Murphy?"

He almost choked, and he hadn't even put any food in his mouth yet. Or touched a utensil. "I've been known to darken the doorway of a church from time to time," he said, though he'd gone a lot more often than that since returning to Coral Canyon. "You?"

"I've been going every week with Beau and Lily, Vi and her boyfriend, Todd."

"And before you didn't?" He finally picked up his fork and knife too, intending on going for the pork first.

"I did when I could," she said. "We toured a lot."

"I'd like to go to church with you," he said. "I've been going to the one downtown. Pastor Franklin says good things, and they run a few youth programs I'm impressed with."

"That's where I've been going," she said, their eyes locking. "Why haven't I seen you there?"

"Let me guess." He cut a piece of pork chop and speared it. "You're one of those people who gets there early and sits in the front." He grinned at her, not at all surprised at the look on her face that said he'd nailed it.

"Well, Beau and Lily get there early and sit in the front," she said. "They're my ride."

"So I'm not as punctual as you—doctors hardly ever are, by the way—and I just slide into the nearest seat so no one notices me." He cocked his head. "Though I haven't seen you either."

"Probably too many cowboy hats blocking your view," she

said, her eyes flicking back to his hat. He honestly felt a bit strange wearing it, but at the same time, it felt like a return to his childhood.

"I wanted to be a cowboy when I was growing up," he said. "They didn't have to wear pressed pants and stuffy shirts with collars that buttoned all the way to their chins." He laughed and shook his head. "My mother was not very keen on that."

"And yet, look at you now." Rose gave him a smoldering look that Liam would've bet money said she wanted to kiss him too, and dropped her eyes to her food.

Liam was hungry to know everything about her, but he was also just plain famished. So he ate, and the conversation was light. She finished long before him, because he kept telling stories about the things he used to do around Coral Canyon as a boy.

Finally, she stood and said, "Should we go downstairs? There's a huge theater room down there."

"Sure." He collected their plates and took them back into the kitchen, placing them in the sink. "Lead on, Miss Everett."

She gave him a sly smile and went first down the steps. He wasn't sure where everyone else in the house had gotten to, but he didn't see anyone in the basement either. There were comfortable couches, another, smaller, kitchen like the one in his summer cabin, and a hallway that led to more doors.

"Bedrooms down here too?" he asked.

"Four, I think," she said, walking past the pool table. "Drinks in the fridge. Hot tub through those doors. Theater room here." She stood in the doorway, framed by only blackness behind her.

Liam's mind lingered a bit too long on the hot tub as he approached her. He took her hand and went in the room first to find a dozen leather recliners. "Nice," he said. "My summer cabin could obviously use an upgrade."

Rose scoffed. "Right. I'm sure it's fabulous."

"Our next date will be at my place, okay? I'll give you the grand tour."

"All right." She exhaled. "Can you cook?"

"Oh, no. Cooking is off the table," he said as his eyes adjusted to the dark. "I mean, I can open cans and stuff. Nothing really edible." Nothing he'd make for his girlfriend.

"I don't suppose you had a lot of ingredients or accommodations where you worked."

"Not a lot, no."

She picked up a stack of DVDs. "You pick." She handed them to him and moved to the very back row, where a loveseat sat nestled in the corner. He watched her curl into the corner, tucking her legs under her skirt and looking at him.

Liam had apparently lost the ability to read, because he looked at the cases blankly. Finally, he just selected one and held it up.

"The player's right there on the wall behind you," she said, and Liam turned to put it in. He knew where he wanted to sit, and the electric current between him and Rose could've lit up New York City for hours.

He loosened his tie and sat on the other half of the loveseat as the screen brightened with the home menu of the movie. They seemed to move as one, perfecting a dance they hadn't even practiced yet.

He lifted his arm, and she slid into his side, making him warm and thrilled at the same time. And now he was ready to watch the movie. He only hoped he could actually pay attention and not spend the next couple of hours entertaining his fantasies.

CHAPTER 9

Rose's heart didn't seem to beat normally once she was curled into Liam's side. She knew deep down in her gut that it was much too early to kiss him. They'd only been out a couple of times, and he had walls between them she wanted removed before anything too terribly intimate—like kissing—could happen.

At the same time, she understood what it was like to have unpleasantries in the past and not want to talk about them. So she couldn't really blame him for keeping his experiences with Doctors Without Borders all bottled up.

So she snuggled with him and watched the movie, laughing at the funny parts and sighing at the romantic ones. When it ended, she practically leapt out of his arms and to her feet. "Okay, I have a surprise."

"Oh, boy," he said with a smile. "I can't wait to see what it is."

"It involves chocolate, and it may or may not be the first time I've attempted this particular dessert." Twice today, actually, and she didn't want to tell him how the first pudding hadn't even set up. She'd followed all of Celia's directions and still the custard had been soup.

Nervousness trickled through her as they left the theater

room and went back upstairs to the kitchen. "It's chocolate." She froze and turned back to him, that loose tie so sexy she wanted to throw herself into his arms and kiss him right now, consequences or not. "You do like chocolate, right?" she asked. "You're not one of those crazy healthy doctors or anything, are you?"

He tipped his head back and laughed, the sound flowing over her and up to the rafters in wonderful waves. She smiled too and giggled.

"I like chocolate," he said, still chuckling.

"Great. So I made this pie, and I hope it'll be good." She moved further into the kitchen and opened the fridge. She'd just finished topping it with whipped cream when he'd knocked on the front door of the lodge. She pulled it out and held it in both hands, gazing at it with wonder streaming through her.

She had not had a normal childhood. Nor a normal adulthood. She had not taken home economics, or learned to cook, or clean, or do hardly anything normal kids and then people did. While Lily and Vi had never hired help in their homes, Rose had.

Back in Nashville, she had a housekeeper and a chef, and plenty of money to pay them. Her mother did too, and she'd always reassured Rose that she wasn't being shallow because she'd rather spend her time at the salon, or the gym, or the mall.

But holding that pie...Rose felt a sense of accomplishment she hadn't known existed. Her double-platinum records did not mean as much as this pie.

Now, she just needed it to taste good. With slightly shaking hands, she set the pie on the counter and got out plates and forks. She wasn't sure how to end this date, because Liam wouldn't be leaving the house. Would they go upstairs together? Would he pause outside her door? Try to kiss her?

Rose's heart could hardly stand the anticipation, and she felt completely out of her element. That was new for her. She'd always been completely in control of her feelings and the relationships she had.

She dictated how fast or slow they went. She'd asked men out before when they'd dragged their feet. She'd taken charge of dates when they started to go badly.

But with Liam…well, Liam was different.

"Are you going to cut it?" he asked, and her eyes flew to his. He watched her with interest, and she wondered how long she'd been standing there.

"Yes." Heat filled her whole body, and her fingers fumbled in the utensil drawer for a knife. Down the hall, Charlie cried, and Rose turned that way. Of course Lily would get him. She and Beau had agreed to have their Valentine's night in their bedroom, where they had a fairly large TV and a mini-fridge. Beau said it was everything he needed.

Sure enough, Charlie quieted in the next moment, and Rose faced Liam again.

"I can do it," he said, gently taking the knife from her. His fingers lingered on hers, and she simply looked at him. "So." He made one long slice down the middle of the pie. "How many kids do you want?"

"What?" Rose almost put one hand over her now-furiously beating heart.

"You want kids, right?" He glanced at her, those oceanic eyes all-knowing. "How many?"

Rose swallowed, her secret out. How he'd known, she wasn't sure. "A lot," she admitted.

"Define 'a lot'." He made another long cut, crossing the first. "I mean, remember the records? Some people would think 'a lot' was one hundred thousand."

"I don't know," Rose said. "I've just always imagined myself with a house full of kids."

Liam nodded, his eyes steadfastly on the pie now. "So in a house like this—or a house like mine—that's a lot of kids. A dozen."

Rose needed to save this conversation. Fast. "Oh, I'm much too old to have a dozen children." She gave a light laugh, hating how fake it felt in her throat. "Even if I started tomorrow, I could probably only have…four."

He lifted his head and looked at her. "Four."

"If I started tomorrow," she said again, taking the knife from him and finishing the job in a few strokes. "Which, obviously, I'm not going to do."

"Obviously."

She put a piece of pie on a plate, and it looked okay. When they both had one, she handed him a fork. "Happy Valentine's Day, Liam."

"Happy Valentine's Day, Rose." They watched one another, the chemistry between them explosive, like God had poured two reactive ingredients together when He'd put Rose and Liam in the same room.

She took a bite of the pie first, and it didn't taste bad. At first. "Oh, no," she said around her mouthful of cream and custard. "Don't eat it." But she probably shouldn't have taken such a big bite, because her words sounded garbled at best.

She tried to wave at Liam, but his motion was already underway and all she ended up doing was flipping cream onto the counter and almost dumping her pie on the floor.

With horror, she watched as he chewed, noting the exact moment he realized the chocolate custard was much too bitter, the crust too crumbly, and the texture not at all smooth the way it should've been.

Rose moved to the sink and put her plate in it before spitting out the offending dessert. "Okay, that was sick." She turned back to Liam who had managed to swallow his. "You ate that?"

He swallowed again, looking around, probably for a drink. Rose hastened to get glasses down from the cupboard and fill them with water. And when Liam started gulping his, she started laughing.

He nearly spit out his water as he joined her. "Well, at least you're not perfect, Rose."

That sobered the moment, and she set her glass on the counter. "You like that I'm not perfect?"

He swept his arm around her waist and drew her close to his body almost like they were slow dancing. He even swayed a little. "Definitely. Who wants to live up to someone who's perfect?"

"Mm," Rose said, closing her eyes and really enjoying this moment in Liam's arms. "I'm starting to get how people feel around you."

He scoffed and stepped back. "Oh, please."

She giggled in a very flirtatious way, and said, "Walk me upstairs, cowboy?" as she laced her hand through his arm.

He did, and he did pause outside her room, gazing down at her with adoration in his eyes. Rose had seen it before. Well, not in such a pair of stunning eyes, and that made the moment all the more powerful.

"Good night. Sorry about the weather." She stretched up and brushed her lips against his cheek before entering her room and closing the door behind her.

She pressed her back into it and took a deep breath. The materials used to redo the lodge were beautiful and expensive, but she could still hear Liam on the other side of the door as he said, "Good night, my beautiful Rose."

––––––––

By the next morning, Mother Nature had blown herself out, leaving behind two feet of snow, downed tree branches, and several reports of people without power, people who'd slid off the road, and people in need.

When Rose arrived, still a bit sleepy and in her pajamas, in the kitchen, she found Beau, Graham, and Liam there, making plans.

"What's going on?" she asked, turning over a mug that had been left by the coffee maker.

Liam filled her in on the help that was needed around Coral Canyon, and she let her eyes slide down his body. "And you're going to go help pull a car out of a snow bank in a suit?"

"I've done a lot in a suit," he said, a devilish twinkle in his eye. "Do you want to come?"

She did, but she didn't at the same time. The lodge still had power, and baby Charlie was home now….

"You should stay here with Lily," Beau said. "She could use the company, and we'll be gone for a long time."

Rose's defenses immediately went up. She could do what she wanted. In the end, though, what she wanted was exactly what Beau had suggested. So she nodded, poured her coffee, and started adding sugar and cream to it.

"I've got the plow on the front of the Hummer," Graham said. "We should be able to get down the canyon."

"It hasn't been plowed?" Rose asked, unable to help herself.

"It's one of the last roads to get done," Graham said. "Especially up this high. They'll go up to the Prospect Lake area first, but then they don't come back until everything else is almost done."

"Don't they know there are people up here?" Rose didn't like the idea of being snowbound, and she'd never had to deal with such a thing in LA or Nashville. Sure, there were a few ice storms or scares in Tennessee every year. Rose simply didn't leave the house, but she could if she wanted to.

"We know to call down if we're having a problem," Graham said. "Come on, guys. I told Sheriff Newbough we'd be down by eight."

Sudden panic seized Rose, and she didn't want any of them to go. "Are you sure it's safe?" Some of her anxiety must have bled into her voice, because all three men stopped what they were doing and looked at her. Beau and Graham looked like they'd had a great, long, full night of sleep. Liam did not. He wore exhaustion around his eyes, and the tie he'd had on last night was completely gone this morning.

"We all have four-wheel drive vehicles," Graham said, glancing first at his brother and then Liam. "I've got the plow, and I'll go first. They'll follow. We'll be all right, Rose."

"What if you're not?" She folded her arms, wishing she was wearing something more commanding than purple silk pajamas.

"I'll call Laney," Graham said. "She'll call the Sheriff. And then I'll call him too."

"And I'll do the same," Beau said. "But I'll call Lily."

"You have a new baby."

Beau gave her a kind smile. "Rose, you're not from Coral Canyon. It snows like this all the time. This is what?" He glanced at Graham. "Our fifth or sixth major storm this winter?"

"At least," Graham said.

Rose looked at Liam. "And you? You've been working in Africa for the last couple of years. I bet it doesn't snow there."

Beau and Graham exchanged a look and scuttled past Rose and down the hall toward the garage. She heard them say something to one another, but she couldn't catch the words.

Liam approached her and put both hands on her shoulders. "I'll be all right." He pressed a kiss to her forehead and made to move past her.

And she didn't like that. Not one little bit. Her concerns were valid, and she'd never liked being brushed off. Her sisters had done it while they wrote songs, until the producers had liked the one Rose had written by herself. Then, suddenly, they'd seen her value. Let her into their inner sanctum. Trusted her.

She did not like watching Liam walk away in those shiny shoes—which had zero traction, thank you very much—and hoping it wouldn't be the last time she saw him.

Behind her, Charlie gave a wail, and Rose spun in that direction. She hurried down the hall to Lily's room and knocked lightly. "It's Rose."

"Come in," Lily said, and Rose pushed into the room to find Lily sitting up in bed with Charlie cradled in her arms. Everything that had been tense and angry inside Rose melted.

"Oh, he's so beautiful," she said as she arrived at the side of the bed. "Can I hold him or are you feeding him?"

"You can hold him and feed him." Lily nodded to the bottle on the bedside table. "I'd love to take a shower."

Rose gently took the tiny infant from her sister and picked up the bottle with a couple of fingers. "We'll be right here. Won't we, sweetheart? Yes, we will." She took Charlie to the rocking recliner and settled down to feed him.

"Did the men leave?" Lily asked.

"Yes," Rose said, some of her earlier discomfort returning. "Will they really be okay?"

Lily glanced up, and their eyes met. "They usually are, Rose."

"Liam has no idea what he's doing," she said. "He barely even listened to me." And she didn't want someone who discounted everything she said just because they were intelligent too. Or because all she'd ever done with her life was write songs.

Rose frowned. She'd never been unhappy with her life—until she came to Coral Canyon. Until she'd seen that there was another type of life possible for her. One with cozy fires, and Christmas traditions, and babies.

She glanced down at Charlie. Oh, how she wanted babies.

Lily trailed her fingers across the top of Rose's head on her way to the bathroom. "Don't think too hard about it, Rose."

She wasn't sure how that related to anything she'd just said, but it probably applied to everything going on in Rose's head. She sighed and rocked, listening to the soothing sound of the shower and the gentle sound of Charlie sucking his bottle.

And this was her new heaven.

Problem was, would Liam even want a life like this? He'd never had it before either, and he didn't seem to be slowing or stopping or even realizing there was something different than what he'd always had.

CHAPTER 10

L iam peered through the windshield, the sunshine making the snow glint wickedly. Graham's plow did quite a good job getting the snow off the road, and Beau's truck put easy-to-follow paths to the pavement. So Liam kept the LandRover on course and foot by foot, mile by mile, the three of them made it down the canyon.

Relief coated his insides, and he flexed his fingers on the steering wheel. He hadn't even realized how tense he'd become. But Rose's anxiety had bled into him, made him question whether he could drive in the snow or not. It *had* been a very long time since he'd had to.

They came upon the first car that needed help getting out of the snowbank on the side of the road. Graham hopped out of his Hummer like he was Wyoming's roadside assistance, and got everything hooked up. Beau worked too, while Liam sat there and watched.

He'd known the Whittaker brothers a little bit growing up. When he took Lars to the swimming holes, the river to fish, or the lake, he'd often see them there too. Graham was a couple of years older than him and Beau a couple younger. But they hadn't been friends.

He admired them now, as they worked for the welfare of others, leaving their warm homes, their wives and children, to come out in the snow and help. Liam had always wanted to help people, so he at least understood that.

He rolled down his window once the car was out and driving off. "I need to go change," he said. "Where should I meet you?"

"The Sheriff is taking volunteers at the station," Beau said. "They've got space heaters and blankets and chicken soup they're taking to anyone who doesn't have power."

"We've got another car a couple of blocks over to get to," Graham said. "We'll meet you over there." He grinned at Liam like they'd be meeting up for a grand time and hopped back in his SUV.

Liam navigated the plowed surface streets in town to go around the block and back up to Prospect Lake. The summer cabin sat at the top of that road, one of the farthest houses along the curve of the lake. Sure enough, it had been plowed all the way up, and he made it into his driveway and garage without too much trouble.

He changed out of the clothes he'd slept in, if it could even be called sleeping. Knowing Rose was just a few doors down, on the same level, had kept him awake for quite a long time. She'd been very clear in her non-verbal communication that she wasn't ready to kiss him.

He wondered why. She'd even admitted to kissing two of the other men she'd dated in the past several months. Why not him?

So he'd tossed and turned and wondered what was so abhorrent about him that she needed to get past. "Maybe she just needs more time," he muttered to himself, same as last night. He put on a pair of jeans he'd barely worn and an undershirt that had seen whiter days. A sweatshirt went over that, and he'd wear his coat too, layering things on the way he'd learned as a boy.

He had a pair of snow boots he'd bought when he'd come to Coral Canyon a month ago, but he'd never truly worn them for longer than it took to haul the trash can to the end of the driveway on Mondays.

Once he was properly geared up, he drove to the Sheriff's station, where dozens of people had shown up to help. He sat in his LandRover and marveled at them. At their small town spirit and how they were there to rally around each other and help.

He wished Rose had come with him, but he didn't want to cause a scene at the lodge. Everyone knew why he'd had to stay over, and while he wasn't ashamed that he was dating Rose, he also didn't want to discuss it with anyone. She'd been upset when he'd left, so he pulled out his phone and typed, *Made it down the canyon okay. Changed and have real boots on now. I'm going to be helping to deliver heaters, food, and blankets to those without heat. Call me later?*

He hit send and got out of the SUV, surprised at how cold the air bit at his nose. That sun sure could be deceiving sometimes. He found Beau and Graham—which wasn't hard as they stood a few inches taller than everyone else—and waited for his turn to get goods and instructions.

"How do you like Rose?" Beau asked, as if he were talking about a new horse Liam had just gotten, or his new car.

Liam gaped at him. "I—"

"Oh, leave him alone," Graham said.

"What?" Beau asked. "She's Lily's sister, and he's obviously interested in her." Beau looked back and forth between Graham and Liam. "Right?"

"Right," Liam said and inched forward. Honestly, was it that hard to grab a list and then move on to get the supplies? He felt like the line should be moving four times as fast as it was.

"It's obviously very new," Graham said in a stage whisper. "Leave him alone."

Liam had never been happier about a purchase before, but his new cowboy hat saved him as he angled his head and turned away from Beau. Then he couldn't see him, and Beau didn't get to look into his eyes either.

"How's the clinic coming?" Graham asked, and Liam was grateful he'd steered the subject away from Rose. Problem was, he didn't want to talk about the clinic either.

"Just fine," he said. "I'm having trouble getting the medical staff I need." He sighed. Maybe he did want to talk about this. Maybe he needed to find a way to talk about things more openly, instead of keeping them hidden, boxed up, private. Hadn't Rose challenged him to do that with his job?

And he hadn't wanted to and hadn't even told her much afterward.

"Coral Canyon is a great place to live," Beau said. "And there are a lot of new houses going in."

"Yeah," Liam said. "But there aren't very many outlying communities to draw from. Like, if I could lure someone from their job in Jackson to here, I think I wouldn't have a problem at all. But if someone works in Jackson, they live there, and they don't want to drive an hour one-way to come here."

"So you're getting brand new people willing to relocate anyway," Graham said.

"I'm trying." Liam finally reached the table and he listened as the curly-haired woman gave him a short list of five people. Names, addresses, phone numbers.

"They all need a heater and blankets," she said. "You'll get those at the next table over. And they all need food. They get a loaf of bread and a container of soup, which is all at the far table. After you've delivered the items, come back here so we can keep track." She smiled, though she'd probably said the same thing dozens of times.

Liam moved to the next table over and started hauling heaters to his LandRover. Fifteen minutes later, he had all the items he needed and he got behind the wheel to see where his people were. Mulberry Street.

Memories washed over him faster than he could close the floodgates. Oh, how he hated Mulberry Street. He and Lars had been riding their bikes home from the swimming hole way out on the east side of town one summer day. Liam had probably been sixteen years old, and certainly big enough to take on the Thompson twins.

But they had slings and rocks, and he'd had to protect his six-year-old brother. He'd ridden down Mulberry Street loads of times over the years, but that summer, Terry Thompson had decided anyone who wanted to use his street had to pay a toll.

And well, Liam thought that was stupid, and illegal, and he wasn't going to pay.

In the end, he'd paid with a black eye and two huge bruises on his legs from where the rocks had hit him. Lars had escaped unscathed, but only because Liam had taken the brunt of the attack. They'd lost their towels in the chaos, and his mother hadn't been happy about that either. She'd packed them up and taken them back to Jackson that evening, straight to the emergency room there.

Liam had been okay. Bruised, not broken. Humiliated, but not terribly hurt. He'd never really told his mother what happened either. Instead, he'd said he'd slipped and fallen when he was running off the rocks that the kids all used to dive into the swimming hole. She hadn't questioned him further.

He'd liked his emergency room doctor, and while he'd been toying with the idea of medical school already, that visit to the ER had solidified his career choice for him.

Then he'd never not know what to do when he got hit with rocks again.

His heart pounded as he rounded the corner onto Mulberry Street. The Thompson's had lived in the house right on the corner, but the name on his list now was Hatch. He pulled into the driveway and collected the items that had been donated.

The front door opened before he'd arrived on the stoop, and it was definitely Mrs. Thompson standing there. She was far older than he remembered, but her dark eyes were the same, as was the way she leaned in the doorway.

"Hello," she said pleasantly. "Thank you so much for

bringing these things." She probably had no idea what her sons had done that day. Or maybe she did. Liam honestly didn't know.

"Shirley Hatch?" he asked, coming up the last of the steps. "I have a heater, some blankets, and some lunch for you."

"Come in, come in." She ushered him inside.

"You are Shirley Hatch?"

"Yes, sir. Right into the kitchen."

It was cold enough in the house for Liam's breath to steam in front of him, and he wasted no time putting the food down and getting the heater set up. "It'll click a bit as the oil inside heats," he said. "I was told that's normal. I was also told that it's best if you put it in a small room and keep the door closed. Maybe I should've put it in the bedroom?"

"No, it's fine here for now," she said. "I'm sure the heat will be back on soon. They're so fast at fixing things these days."

"Hmm." Liam couldn't help looking around the living room, which connected to the dining room and kitchen. There were no photos on the mantel, nor the walls. Not one.

Odd, he thought. "Have you always lived here, ma'am?" he asked.

"For fifty years now," she said with a touch of pride in her voice.

"I knew…well, I thought some twins lived here. About my age?"

"Yes," she said with delight. "My sons." Her face fell. "Well, they used to live here."

Liam wanted to ask where they'd gone and if they'd still sling rocks at him if he tried to ride his bicycle down Mulberry Street. But he didn't have to.

Mrs. Hatch continued with, "They left years ago. Have never been back." She moved over to the counter where he'd set the food and opened the twist tie on the loaf of bread.

"Where did they go?" he asked.

"With their dad. I guess they really did love him more than

me, and when they were forced to choose, they chose him. None of 'em have been back in at least twenty-five years."

Twenty-five years. The incident with the slings had happened almost exactly twenty-five years ago.

"I'm so sorry," Liam said, and he meant it. His training with Doctors Without Borders had taught him sympathy and empathy and how to be sincere about both.

"Oh, it's fine," Mrs. Hatch said. "This soup is already hot, so I don't need electricity to warm it up. And I'll be fine with the blankets and the heater."

Liam cocked his head slightly, wondering if Mrs. Hatch was as sound in mind as she'd been previously. "Well, I have other deliveries to get to." He tipped his hat to her, another good reason to wear the cowboy hat everyday, and headed for the door.

"Thank you again," she called after him, and Liam escaped the house. He glanced to the corner where the first rock had sailed from, and then he got the heck out of there. He didn't want to relive those memories. Go through those feelings again. Talk about anything uncomfortable. The Murphy's had never done that, and Liam didn't want to start now.

His phone chimed as he climbed in his SUV to go to the next house. *How's it going?* Rose asked.

It was as if the sky had opened again, only this time instead of snow, there was a heavenly choir of angels singing—and Liam knew.

If he wanted to be with Rose, really be hers and have her be his, he'd have to share things with her. Good things, sure. But bad things too. He'd never done that before, and that was why he'd never felt close to any of the women he'd dated in the past.

So he had two choices. Open up to Rose, or cut her loose.

And the thought of never seeing her again—never getting to kiss her—had his heart in knots and his stomach jumping with nerves.

He tapped out, *I just had to take some stuff into a house of a couple of boys who threw rocks at me—literally—when I was a kid. It was horrible. Tell you all about it later,* and hit send before driving next door for the next delivery.

A sense of freedom filled his soul, and the rest of the deliveries went without a hitch. And with so many people helping, by the time he returned to the Sheriff's station, all the names and supplies had been assigned.

Can you leave that baby long enough to go to lunch with me? he texted, adding a smiley emoji to the end of it, so she'd know he wasn't upset about her loving her nephew.

Of course, she responded. *Are you driving all the way back up here to get me?*

Of course, he texted, already with more bounce in his step. So it freaked him out that Rose wanted four kids. They didn't have to decide right now. In fact, he needed to kiss her first before any major decisions were made, and he wasn't even sure that would happen today.

But he was hoping. And praying couldn't hurt either, he decided as he made the turn to head back up to Whiskey Mountain Lodge.

CHAPTER 11

R ose carefully laid a sleeping baby Charlie in his bassinet and tiptoed out of Lily and Beau's room. She found them in the living room, Lily's head in Beau's lap with her eyes closed. He stroked her hair and smiled softly at Rose as she paused in the hallway.

"The baby's asleep too," she whispered.

"Thank you, Rose." Beau leaned his head back and closed his eyes too, and Rose wanted to take a mental snapshot and hold onto it forever. This was what love looked like. What a family looked like. What everything Rose wanted looked like.

She turned away from Beau and Lily and went into the kitchen, pinching pains in her chest. She hadn't waited as long as Lily to have children; she still had time. She told herself this over and over as she paced from one kitchen counter to the other.

Liam was on his way back up to the lodge, and Rose felt the things she needed to say to him building under her tongue. *Do you want children? You never said….*

How many do you want?

Will you ever listen to me if I have concerns about things? Or will you just do what you want, when you want?

It was better for her to know the answers to these things now, before she got in too deep with him. At the same time, she feared she already was in way over her head, and breaking the surface so she could breathe was still a long way off.

Text me when you get here, she sent to him, suddenly thinking of it. *Lily and Beau are asleep in the front room, and I don't want to wake them.*

Will do.

Rose stepped into the mudroom and put on her coat. She'd been using the deep eggplant puffy coat to go out with Daisy from time to time, and it would do for lunch. The sidewalks had been cleared, and she walked up to the crest of the small hill and looked into the bare branches of the trees.

The wind had completely died, and it was so, so silent. Rose wasn't sure she'd ever heard something so still, and so quiet.

"Am I doing the right thing with Liam?" she whispered into the brilliant, blue sky, thinking that if there was anywhere on Earth to be closer to God than right here, she'd never find it.

The breeze picked up, and she swore she heard a definite *yes* whispering through the limbs. She turned and headed around the side of the lodge to the front, where she could wait for Liam and not wake her family.

She huddled on the porch, out of the reach of the wind, and the view on this side of the lodge was just as spectacular. The road was a black slash among all the white snow, and wound down the mountain until it disappeared.

Trees stretched for miles and miles, and Rose took a deep, cleansing breath and said another prayer as Liam's SUV came up the hill and into the parking lot. Her heart thumped in an irregular beat, and she was actually happy about it. She hoped she'd always be as excited to see him as she was right now.

He pulled under the overhang and rolled down the passenger window. "I'm here," he said with a smile, moments before Rose pulled open the door and got in.

"It is freezing out there," she said, her lower jaw shaking slightly. "Does this thing have a seat warmer?"

"Right here, sweetheart." He pushed a button and three orange lights glowed to life.

"Thanks." She grinned at him, noting he wore the cowboy hat again today, and he'd paired it with jeans and a sweatshirt, over which he wore his winter coat. Yet again, another completely different look than she'd seen on him before. And she still liked it.

Sweetheart echoed through her mind, and she buckled her seatbelt and held her cold fingers in front of the vent. "Where are we going for lunch?"

"There's a great salad bar over in Dog Valley."

Rose looked at him out of the corner of her eye as he got the SUV moving. "Dog Valley? And where is that?" Her stomach tightened, as she hadn't eaten breakfast that morning after the mini-confrontation about going out in the snow to help people while wearing patent leather shoes.

But he wasn't wearing those shoes now.

"It's a little town about thirty minutes northeast of here," he said. "You'll love it. There's this gift shop-slash-drugstore that has awesome stuff."

Rose giggled, wishing she didn't sound so young when she did it. "Awesome stuff? That is so specific."

"You know, like notebooks and cute pens and cards and oh! There's a soda fountain."

"It sounds like the owner doesn't know what kind of store they have."

"It's amazing. Trust me."

She wanted to trust him, and she did trust God, so she reached across the console between them and laced her fingers through his. "Liam, did it—were you freaked out when I said I wanted to have a lot of kids?"

"Honestly?"

"If we're not going to be honest with each other, you might as well take me back to the lodge right now." Rose couldn't believe she'd said the words, but they were just there. And she did mean them.

He gave her a look and smiled. "Good point. After all, you'd like to start having kids tomorrow."

"Technically, that would be today, and we both know that's not going to happen."

"No?"

"Liam." She rolled her eyes. "We haven't even kissed yet."

"Is that going to happen today?" He squeezed her hand.

"I don't know," Rose said. "I haven't decided yet."

"Who says you get to decide?"

She looked at him, finding the playfulness in his eyes though he only took them off the road for half a second. "Whatever, cowboy." She added a laugh to it, but the truth was, she wanted to kiss Liam. Badly. She just didn't want to bear the scar on her heart forever if things didn't work out with them.

In that moment, she realized she was almost desperate for one of her relationships to finally make it past the exciting, dating, first-kiss stage. Very few had in the last couple of years, and with Vi and Lily finding their forever partner, Rose very much wanted to as well.

And no, she wasn't getting any younger to have those kids she wanted.

"You never answered my question," she said, deciding not to let this go. She'd felt good about it in the backyard, whether the wind had whispered to her or not.

"Yes," he said. "Honestly, yes, Rose. It freaked me out a little bit. I've...." He flexed his fingers around the steering wheel, removed his hand from hers to make a turn in the canyon, and cleared his throat. "I've never wanted kids."

"Ever?" Horror struck Rose behind all twenty-four ribs.

"Ever," he said. "I worked with a lot of kids in Africa, and they're great. I've just never wanted to be a dad. I guess...." He trailed off and looked out the window, both hands solidly on the wheel now.

Rose mourned the loss of his skin touching hers, and she realized how difficult this conversation was for him. She let him drive, not pushing him to finish. He would, when he was ready.

Finally, he said, "I guess I just never thought of myself as father material." He looked at her for what felt like a long time before focusing on the windy road again. "My dad was never home, and I hardly knew him. I don't want to be that kind of dad, and I've always worked more than he did."

Rose felt something very final in his words, but she didn't know what it meant. "But you don't have to work as much as you do. Right?"

"To get the clinic open? Absolutely I do. I don't do as much as needs to be done."

"But just right now." After all, they wouldn't be married and on their way to having a family for months. Probably a year. Maybe longer than that. Rose shook her head. Her thoughts were crazy. She'd met Liam just over a month ago, and just because he was dashingly handsome, with dreamy blue eyes, and a fancy doctor's coat didn't mean she was in love with him.

In fact, he'd hardly shared anything of himself with her. "Tell me about the kids who threw rocks," she said.

"Rose," he said, his voice heavy with emotion. "I do have to work a lot, right now and always. Emergency medical clinics don't run themselves."

"Of course they don't." People hired managers. But she somehow knew Liam wouldn't do that. She folded her arms and looked out the window, a perfect storm of disappointment rotating around with hope that made a cyclone inside her chest that hurt. Hurt, badly.

"So one summer when I was about sixteen, I took my brother to this swimming hole on the other side of town…." Liam told the story of riding their bikes, swimming all day, and then getting ready to go home.

"When we got to Mulberry Street, the Thompson twins had set up a booth for a bicycle toll. I wasn't going to pay that, so

Lars and I rode on by. The twins launched rocks at us all the way down the road. It was awful. I took a heater and some supplies to their mother today. She says they haven't been back in twenty-five years."

"Wow," Rose said. "That's a sad story on a lot of levels."

"Isn't it?"

"What did your mother do?"

"What do you mean?"

"I'm sure she said something to their mother."

"You think so?" He looked at her.

"I would've."

"She took me and Lars back to Jackson Hole, and I went to the emergency room." He fell silent for a few minutes. "It was then I decided I wanted to become a doctor. And you're right. My mom took Lars and left for a while. My dad was there to take me home after the doctor finished with the x-rays and everything." He looked thoughtful as they came out of the canyon and into Coral Canyon.

He turned right and then left to get on the main highway that led back to Jackson Hole, but they only stayed on it for a few miles. Once he'd made another right turn toward Dog Valley and another town named Chester, she said, "Sounds like you protected Lars, though."

"I did," he said. "I feel like I've spent my whole life protecting Lars. Well, until I left for Geneva, for my first Doctors Without Borders assignment."

"So you're not very close with your family."

"I mean, yes? No? I don't know. My work kept me away for years, so...."

"No, Liam," Rose said carefully, not wanting to freak him out for a second time in twenty-four hours. "*You* kept you away. We all make choices."

Several long seconds passed, and he said, "I know, Rose. You're right." The rest of the drive to Dog Valley happened seemingly in the blink of an eye. Rose even wondered if she'd fallen asleep.

"Stay there," Liam said, hopping out of the SUV and hurrying around the front. He opened her door for her, but stepped into the new space created so she couldn't get out. Was he going to kiss her now? In the freezing cold weather, with wind, in a place called Dog Valley?

Rose looked up at him, but before she could say anything, he said, "I'm trying to be more open with you, Rose. Okay? I'm trying."

She got out of the SUV and right into his personal space. "You're doing great, Liam." She balanced herself by putting her hands on his shoulders. "You said that kids freak you out. You work too much, and you had a bad childhood experience on Mulberry Street. I think you've done very well today."

He finally grinned, the anxiety in his beautiful eyes extinguishing. "Well enough to get a kiss?"

She laughed and slapped him on the chest, though it did nothing through the thick fabric of his coat. "Come on, cowboy. I'm starving. And I can't be thinking about kissing when I'm hungry."

CHAPTER 12

L iam took Rose's hand as they walked into the pizza joint. "So you are at least thinking about kissing me then."

She paused at the door and looked at him, those gorgeous blue eyes all sparkly when she said, "Oh, Liam. Don't you know every woman thinks about kissing you the moment they lay eyes on you?" She patted his chest like he was a fun puppy and entered the building. He wasn't sure if he should laugh or scoff or go get in the SUV and leave her there.

The door slammed closed only a couple of inches from his face, making him jolt. Something hot burned in his blood, and he hurried after her. She stood in line, her eyes fixed on the menu. "It's a buffet?"

"You can get an all-you-can-eat salad bar, yes," he said. "Or pizza too. I'll probably get both." He moved right into her personal space, thrilled when she leaned against his body like she hadn't just said every female in the world wanted to kiss him. But if that meant she did….

He couldn't stop thinking about kissing her, and he drew in a deep breath of her hair, wondering if he could do it right there in line at the Pizza Pals in Dog Valley.

Absolutely not, he told himself. Rose Everett was a sophisticated woman who wore blouses made of the finest silks. She wouldn't want their first kiss to be in a pizzeria that served a lunch buffet seven days a week for ten bucks.

So he kept her close, breathing in the baby powdery scent of her skin and the strawberry quality of her hair. They both got salad and pizza buffets, and Liam wondered if this would be a trend for them.

When he asked her, she said, "There are worse things to do together," and took another bite of her Hawaiian Alfredo pizza. "And this place is way better than the one in Coral Canyon."

Liam thought so too, and he was glad they'd had time to get together today. His to-do list for the clinic was miles long, but he told himself it would still be there tomorrow.

"So I did learn a lot working for Doctors Without Borders," he said.

Her eyes lit up and she put her pizza down. "Oh?"

Her interest in his life baffled him, but he forged on anyway. "Yeah. That there will always be more work to do. More people to see. Another day to do it, and see them."

She cocked her head a bit. "And is that good or bad?"

"I think it's good. Helped me realize that what I don't get done today, I can do tomorrow."

"Ah, the ultimate in procrastination."

"Or, a liberating way of playing hooky for the day so I can spend more time with you."

"Yes, I like that better." She grinned and picked up her pizza slice again. "So what are we doing after this? Why is this town called Dog Valley?"

"They have one of the biggest animal sanctuaries in the country here," he said. "Wyoming has been a no-kill state for dogs for a while now, because of Dog Valley."

"Fascinating," Rose said. "I want to see the sanctuary. Can we tour it or something?"

"We sure can." He woke his phone and started tapping. "Let's see what they've got for this afternoon." He tapped and typed, swiped and scrolled. "Looks like we can get on the three o'clock bus."

"Let's do it."

He filled in the info required, tapped a few more times, and it was done. "All right. We're set." He smiled at her and reached for his soda.

"Are you sure?" she asked.

"Yeah, I've done it before. It's fun."

"That's not what I meant." Rose wore a serious look, and it was almost as exciting as her playful ones. "I don't want to keep you from work if you have things to do."

"Rose." He reached across the table and took both of her hands in his. "There will always be things to do. Now come on." He stood up and put his coat back on. "I believe I promised you an amazing gift shop, and we have a few hours to fill anyway."

"You think it will take hours to look around a drugstore?"

"I sure do."

He laughed as she said, "Wow, this place better be amazing, because you've talked it up so much, I'm actually excited."

It was a short drive down the road and around a curve to the Dog Valley Drug, and Liam knew the moment they walked inside that they'd be there at least an hour.

Rose paused, sucked in a breath, and said, "Oh my gosh. Look at those notebooks." Her eyes shone with glee as they looked at him and then back to the rack of notebooks in every shape, size, and color. They had ones that laid flat, some with dogs on the front, and sparkly, tall ones that were a couple of inches wide and a couple thick that said UNICORNS EXIST in huge letters.

"I have to have this," she said, picking up the unicorn pad.

"Of course you do," he said, chuckling. "Or what about this one?" He picked up a teal notebook that said BELIEVE on the front of it in red glitter. "It's like a Christmas list-making book."

"Yep, getting that." She plucked it from his fingers and looked around. "Do they have carts here?"

———

BY THE TIME THEY FINISHED AT THE DRUGSTORE, LIAM HAD EATEN way too much ice cream and Rose had spent way too much money on notebooks, earrings, and funny cards. They'd gone on to the animal sanctuary, where they'd both bought sweatshirts while they waited for the tour to begin, and now Rose was standing in one of the dog buildings, chewing her nails.

"Are you *sure* your sister and brother-in-law will let you bring a dog back to the lodge?" Liam asked, and not for the first time.

Rose hadn't seemed to hear him—truly hear him—the first five times. She went over to another door. "Buttercup's just so cute," she said at the white bulldog who kept all four feet on the floor and didn't make a sound.

The worker who'd been with them for at least thirty minutes said, "I can send you home with a list of dogs. It'll give you a decent idea of their personalities, their medical histories as much as we know, and their adoption fees."

Since that was done on weight and medical conditions, every dog was different. And the Dog Valley animal sanctuary was appropriately located, because there were over four hundred dogs to choose from, all looking for forever homes.

Rose had narrowed it down by breed and size, and she was currently looking for a dog a bit bigger than forty pounds, because then the adoption fee would be waived. As if she didn't have the money to adopt every dog in this sanctuary, and feed them, and care for their medical needs.

Liam certainly did, and she must have much more money than he did.

She turned back to him. "Maybe I should get two. Then they won't be lonely once they come home with me."

"Rose." Liam shook his head. "You live in a room on the second floor of a lodge you don't own. Maybe you should talk to Lily and Beau first." She hadn't sent a text or made a call to his knowledge. "And maybe you should get your own place in town."

He pulled in a slow breath when he realized what he'd said. "I mean—"

"You think I should get my own place in town?" she asked, abandoning her quest to find a new pet.

"I'm going to go get the list," the worker said smartly, and she got the heck out of the dog enclosure.

"I mean, yeah." Liam shrugged, this whole tell-her-how-he-felt thing not going so well. He had told her a bit about his childhood, and a little more about his work. But talking about his feelings for her was a whole new ballgame. "Are we just playing a game here?"

"No," she said quickly.

"And you don't have to be in Nashville, right?"

"Right."

"I mean, you don't *have* to go back there."

"I have a house there. Of course I have to go back."

"Permanently? Or to sell the place?" Liam was stunned at his own boldness. He stepped into Rose and took her into his arms before he lost it. "Because I want you to stay in Coral Canyon. With me, Rose Everett. I want you to stay in Coral Canyon and give us a chance." He commanded himself to stop talking, though there were more words pressing against the back of his tongue.

He swallowed them away and looked at her. "What do you think?"

She gazed up at him, so many things running through her eyes he couldn't categorize them all.

"What do I think?" she said, leaning into him further. "I think I'm going to kiss you now."

Surprise shot through Liam, and he murmured, "In a dog shelter? This is where you want our first kiss to be?"

Her eyes, which had been drifting closed, burst open again. Liam kicked himself for saying anything.

"I mean, I'm an idiot. Let's have that kiss."

She laughed and pushed against his chest. "No, you're right. This isn't romantic, nor will we ever be able to come back here and replicate the moment."

"Oh?" Liam grinned at her, a measure of idiocy still running through him. "Is that something we'll have to do?"

"I mean, if we can." She shrugged and headed for the exit. "I think it's romantic, don't you?"

He thought whatever she thought. "Sure," he said.

The worker met them outside, a thick sheaf of papers in her hand. "We're open seven days a week. Eight to five."

"Thanks." Rose gave her an appreciative smile, and she and Liam got back in the SUV. She remained quiet on the way back to Coral Canyon, and Liam let it stay that way. He had a lot of thoughts going on inside his mind too, and he was trying to decide if he wanted their first kiss to be on the porch of the lodge.

A lodge neither of them owned and probably wouldn't visit all that much once Rose bought her own house.

Bought her own house. Had he really said that to her? Out loud?

In a dog enclosure.

Sometimes he really wondered how he'd made it through medical school, because sometimes he wasn't all that smart.

He didn't want to kiss her in the SUV, and did he walk her to the door after a simple lunch date? Liam had no idea what to do. So he just drove with a prayer streaming through his mind and heart, and when he finally pulled to Whiskey Mountain Lodge, Rose turned to him and asked, "Would you like to come in for coffee?" he couldn't get out of the SUV fast enough.

The lodge was warm and smelled like a cut of beef had been stewing all day. He'd barely closed the door behind him when Rose turned and put both palms on his chest. "Okay, I can't do it."

"Do what?"

Instead of answering, she tipped up on her toes, her eyes drifting closed, a clear invitation for him to kiss her right there, right then.

This time, Liam didn't suggest that a more romantic location should be found. He slipped his arms around her, closed his eyes, and bent down to meet her halfway. The moment their lips touched, bright lights flashed in his vision.

She melted into him, pressing closer, and Liam held onto her and kissed her properly, thinking they fit together so well that she'd been made to kiss him.

CHAPTER 13

Rose had kissed several men, and not one of them made her feel as loved and cherished as Liam did. In fact, she wasn't sure she'd ever been kissed properly before this. She didn't seem to be able to stand on her own volition, and he held her tight against him so it didn't matter.

She wasn't sure how long she kissed him, only that she didn't want to stop.

Someone cleared their throat in a loud, obvious way, and Rose jumped apart from Liam, spinning toward the sound, which had come from behind her. Lily stood there, a very Mom-like look on her face. She quirked one eyebrow and folded her arms. "Hey, guys."

Embarrassment crawled up Rose's spine, as if she'd indeed been caught kissing the guy from the wrong side of the tracks by her mother. She let her long hair fall in front of her face, and she noticed Liam standing halfway behind her.

"Hey," she said, lifting her chin. "Liam was just leaving."

"I can see that." Lily's face burst into a smile. "I'd really like to see what he's like when he's arriving."

A breath happened, and then Lily and Liam started laughing

at the same time. Rose couldn't help smiling too, but she was still too warm and woozy from that kiss—oh, that kiss—and she reached for the railing of the steps that went up to the second floor to steady herself.

"I think you invited me in for coffee," he said, slipping his arm effortlessly around her.

Rose tilted her head to look up at him. Didn't he know that was a ploy to get him inside so she could kiss him? His eyes searched hers, and she concluded that, nope. He'd thought it was an invitation for coffee.

"All right," she said. "Can we make coffee?" She looked at Lily for permission.

"And you wanted to bring home a dog," he whispered. "*Two* dogs. Over forty pounds *each*."

"Sh," she said, keeping her eyes on Lily.

"Sure," she said. "I don't care. I was just coming to get a bowl of ice cream."

"I'll take that instead," Liam said, and he moved down the single step from the entryway and into the living room. Rose watched him move with effortless grace, and it was clear he'd charmed Lily too.

But it was Rose he'd kissed. She touched her lips, the next time she could kiss him so very far away. Her heartbeat settled into a normal rhythm, and she went to join her sister and her boyfriend for ice cream in the dead of winter.

———

SHE DIDN'T SEE LIAM THE NEXT DAY, OR THE NEXT. APPARENTLY HE worked weekends too, but they'd agreed to meet for church on Sunday morning. Rose had escaped any lectures about kissing too soon or the wrong man by Lily, for which she thanked her lucky stars each day.

She still got to hold baby Charlie, and Celia had disposed of the disgusting pie from Valentine's Day. Rose used to spend all her time writing songs and plucking strings, and she hadn't done either since arriving in Coral Canyon.

So when she got back to the notebooks full of lyrics she'd scrawled over the years, her eyes seemed to pick out the exact ones she should use. A new song came together in a matter of an hour, and she drove down the canyon to Vi's on Saturday afternoon to borrow some of her instruments.

The house was perfectly ordinary, sitting in a regular neighborhood like Vi had never stood on a stage with six spotlights on her as she sang the prettiest ballad the sisters had. She'd said she wouldn't be home, so Rose went right in, almost falling backward when Vi said, "Hey, Rose."

A yelp came out of her mouth, and she dropped her car keys. "Vi." She pressed one hand over her heart as she found her sister sitting on the couch a few feet from the front door. "You said you wouldn't be home."

"Yeah, I didn't think I would be. But Todd wanted to go snowshoeing and it hurts my hips. So." She indicated the Old English sheepdog next to her. "I got Jetstream and there's hot chocolate in the kitchen."

"I'll take some of that," Rose said, entering the house and closing the door. "And hey, you can tell me if this song is stupid or not."

"Sure." Vi got up and tucked her short hair behind her ear, where of course, it didn't stay.

"No engagement ring yet?" Rose asked as they moved into the kitchen for the treats first.

"No," she said darkly. "Honestly, I don't know what he's waiting for. We didn't go out on Valentine's Day because of the storm, but we did the next night. Nothing." Vi heaved a huge sigh, and Rose felt her disappointment through her whole body.

"I'm sorry, Vi." She took the mug her sister gave her. "Want me to say something to him?"

"Absolutely not. Lily keeps asking too. It's fine. It'll happen when it happens."

"He knows you want to get married in the spring. Maybe he just doesn't want a long engagement."

"What's the difference?" Vi asked sourly. "And if I was wearing a ring, maybe I'd be more inclined to move the date up. Maybe I wouldn't want to wait if I thought he really wanted me."

Rose paused, hearing the self-depreciation in her sister's voice. "Vi," she said carefully. "Of course he wants you. He flew to Nashville and broke into your house to get you back, remember?"

"Not technically," she said. "Lily gave him the codes." She put more mini marshmallows in her hot chocolate than fit, and several spilled out the top. She didn't bother to pick them up. "Anyway." She drew in a deep breath through her nose. "I hear you've been being a little naughty."

"Oh, I have not." Rose waved her hand like she was swatting away a fly.

"So you didn't kiss Liam Murphy at the lodge?"

"I did, yes," Rose said, that same wonderful heat crawling through her again as the memory entered her mind. A smile came with it and she let her hair fall between her and Vi. "But we weren't being naughty. It was a kiss, and last time I checked, I'm thirty-five-years-old and allowed to kiss men." Especially when they were as handsome as Liam. "But maybe I need my own place...."

Vi giggled and picked up her lost marshmallows. "That you do, baby sister. That you definitely do." She gave Rose a devilish look. "Then you can kiss him whenever you want, and I won't have to tell Lily that you're not moving too fast."

Rose almost slopped the hot water over the back of her hand. "Is that what she said?"

"Something like that. I don't remember exactly. She said she was worried about you, because you think you own him? Something like that."

"I do not," Rose said, mildly horrified. "I paid for him in the auction, sure, but that was our Valentine's Day date. Everything else is just…us."

"A perk," Vi said, grinning. "I mean, I've seen him. He's very good looking."

"He's not a perk, Vi," Rose said. "He's a person. I like him." She met her sister's eyes, almost choking on the desperation. "I like him so much. *Too* much."

Vi covered Rose's hand with hers, and it was warm from holding the hot chocolate mug. "Maybe that's what Lily means. That you go too fast."

Rose gave her a small smile, the panic beginning to bleed away. "You're the one who falls in love too fast, remember?" She nudged her gently.

"I know," Vi said. "And see where it's gotten me? Sitting on the couch with my boyfriend's dog, no diamond on my finger, and wondering when my life is going to begin."

Rose almost laughed, then she realized that Vi was being serious. "He's going to ask you, Vi. I mean, I've seen you two together. He's mad for you."

Vi sighed again, reaching into the bag for more marshmallows. "I know." She nodded. "Yeah, I know."

Rose added the chocolate powder to her hot water and started stirring. "So let's focus on songs today, and men later, okay?"

"Okay." Vi gave her a quick smile and said, "I bet you included a banjo part, and I happen to have mine from Nashville."

"Of course there's a banjo part." Rose scoffed like anything less would be ridiculous. Which, for her, it would be. "How's the house selling going in Nashville?"

"Not great," Vi said. "Calvin says not to worry. We need a special kind of buyer. Blah, blah, blah." Vi took her mug and left the kitchen. "Are you going to list your place?"

"I'm thinking about it," she said.

"Ask Mom and Dad to do it," Vi said. "They're thinking of selling too."

"What? Really?" Rose followed Vi down the hallway and into a bedroom she'd converted into her music room. Her piano from Nashville sat in the corner, and her guitars and other instruments sat in their holders or hung on the wall.

"Really. It's killing her that she's not here for Lily and to see Charlie. They're coming next weekend." Vi sat on one of the chairs in the room. "Dad's ready to retire. We all live here. They should move here."

"We don't all live here permanently." Rose put her hot chocolate on the windowsill, thinking it would cool faster so she could drink it. She opened her bag and started digging for her notes and the sheet music.

"You just said you were going to get your own place," Vi said.

"I know. But it's not permanent. I mean, I've kissed the guy once, and now he's too busy to see me again." The words just slipped out of Rose's mouth, but they vocalized all her fears about her and Liam's relationship.

Vi watched her but said nothing.

"Okay," Rose said, shaking off the bad vibes she felt. She didn't need any of that infecting her while she was trying to make music. "So this song is about a woman who's lost in a storm. But really it's her mind." She spread the music on the piano and positioned herself on the bench.

Her fingers found the chords and progressions naturally, though she hadn't played in a long, long time. She loved playing the piano, and she missed it. She missed the mild winters in Nashville. She missed her parents. And most of all, she missed writing songs and singing them with her sisters.

So when Vi got up and peered over her shoulder before turning to get an acoustic guitar, a happiness Rose hadn't experienced for a while descended over her. And when Vi strummed and hummed, then started to sing with Rose, everything in the world was okay.

Even Liam working long hours and forgetting to text her before he went to bed.

CHAPTER 14

Liam studied the plans with the construction manager, the hard hat he'd been forced to wear pinching against his forehead. "It looks fine," he said.

"It adds two weeks to the schedule," Paul said. "And I know you want the clinic open as fast as possible. But with the weather the way it's been, and the safety issues this cause…." He let the words hang there, and while Liam didn't like them, he didn't see another way.

"It's okay," he said, clapping the man on the shoulder. "We need operational pipes. I'll just have to have a little talk with Mother Nature about all this snow." He put a smile on his face, and it felt eerily like the ones he used to wear in Nigeria. He'd always been jovial with his patients though they were facing some of the worst health problems of their lives.

He remembered the pure exhaustion he'd felt by the time he'd returned to his tent. He was feeling that here in Coral Canyon too, and he didn't like it.

His phone rang and he turned away from Paul with an, "Excuse me." The name on the phone got his pulse racing, and he swiped open the call and kept walking. "Hey, Arthur."

Dr. Gurnsey had to have good news for him. He simply had

to. Liam held his breath and sent up a quick prayer as Arthur said, "Afternoon, Liam," in his deep, bass voice.

Liam watched the wind blow wispy snow across the parking lot beyond the glass double doors. "How are things in Lansing?" He knew it was a big move for the man, who had a wife and three kids.

Three kids. Liam shook his head, wondering if he'd ever feel like he could be a family man.

"Cold," Arthur said with a chuckle.

"Well, they're not much better here," Liam said, wanting to be upfront with the man. He'd met Arthur first in medical school, where they'd done a residency together. Their paths had separated and come back together in Washington for about six months before Liam left that hospital in favor of Doctors Without Borders. Arthur had stayed for another few years, and then he'd moved to Lansing.

He was the best general practitioner Liam knew, and he'd been talking to him for months about coming to Coral Canyon and heading up the clinic.

"It snowed about two feet just a couple of days ago." The drifts weren't going anywhere either, as the temperatures kept them frozen solid.

"I'd like to come tour the facility," Arthur said. "Is it done enough to do that?"

Liam turned back to the open area behind him. "Yeah, it is. Tell me when, and I'll make it happen." He'd have to talk to Pearl Wiley, the hospital administrator, which he didn't particularly like doing. He understood that it was her job to make sure all the red tape got cleared, but she always presented problems for Liam's great ideas.

"What about next week?"

"Oh, so soon," Liam said. "Yeah, that should be fine." More and more supplies were arriving each day, and while he'd gotten signed contracts from four nurses, they didn't actually start until the clinic opened.

So Liam had been organizing and putting things away, making phone calls, meeting with contractors, and Pearl, and other potential staff candidates. He'd met with maintenance at the hospital and made a plan, and there was still so much to do.

"I'm bringing Kami and the kids."

So Arthur was serious. "That's great," Liam said. "I know some locals that can show them around." Well, Rose and Vi weren't exactly locals, but the Whittakers were, and Laney, and even Vi's boyfriend had grown up in town.

Liam tried not to get his hopes up. It was common practice for doctors to come take tours, bring their families, all of it, before they took a new job. But it was certainly a step in the right direction, and Liam ended the call more hopeful than he'd been all week.

Just got great news, he texted to Rose. He'd been thinking about her constantly, and had even typed out a few texts inviting her to just come sit with him down at the clinic. Just be in the same space with him.

But it was cold here, and she'd have nothing to do, and he'd erased the texts, put his head down, and kept working.

She didn't respond, and he wondered what she was doing that afternoon. Maybe rocking baby Charlie, or maybe she'd come down to town with her sisters, or maybe she'd gone shopping in Jackson Hole.

Liam looked at his clipboard and sighed. He still needed an office manager, as well as two more doctors to staff the clinic. And he needed to meet with Veronica and Pearl about the auction funds, and there was a grant from the state of Wyoming he needed to follow up with.

So he retreated to the office just outside the clinic that the hospital had provided for him. It was at least warm, and it contained everything he needed to get some work done. Electricity, a computer, all his files and notes, and a coffee maker.

He'd just logged into his account to check the grant when someone said, "Knock, knock." He turned to find Pearl standing there. Though it was Saturday, she wore a crisp, navy skirt suit with matching heels.

Liam jumped to his feet. "Hello, Pearl." He shook her hand and fell back. Of course, his phone chose that moment to crackle out Rose's notification sound, but Liam didn't let himself look at the device. "What can I do for you?"

"Just checking to see how things are going."

Liam sent her weekly reports, and admittedly, he hadn't yet this week. It had been a somewhat strange week, with the auction on Monday night, the huge Valentine's Day storm and subsequent clean up soon after that, all the time he'd spent with Rose....

He leaned against the countertop that served as his desk. "I was just going to send you the report," he said. "I've been in and out this week, but I just met with Paul." He continued to detail the slight plumbing setback due to the freezing conditions, and the phone call with Arthur.

"Arthur Gurnsey?" she asked, as if she'd never heard the name before. But Liam had met with her and they'd gone over a list of potential candidates for the doctorial positions. She'd had to personally approve each one.

As the emergency clinic would operate under her direction, Liam understood. Sort of. It wasn't hospital owned, but simply housed on the grounds. Still, he'd done everything he could to satisfy Pearl Wiley, because she could literally make or break the success of the clinic.

And Liam wanted it to succeed so badly.

Why is that? The question floated across his mind, but he didn't have an answer for it.

"Yes," he said. "Arthur Gurnsey. He's bringing his wife and kids out next week for a tour of the place. I was just going to ask your availability." He indicated the open laptop beside him.

"Whenever he's here, I can be available," she said, indicating that she wanted Arthur badly too. He had been their top recruit for a while now.

"I'll keep you updated."

"When did you talk to him?"

"Maybe a half an hour ago?" His phone crackled again, and he reached for it to silence it. "I was just going over the Rural Medical Grant as well, to see where we are with that, and we need to meet with Veronica for the funds from the auction."

Pearl softened the tiniest bit. "I was there that night, you know."

"Oh?" Liam picked up his clipboard, wondering what he could push to another day, because he really wanted to see Rose that evening. Sure, they'd agreed to meet at church the following morning, but that felt so far away. And he couldn't kiss her the way he wanted to at church.

"You fetched *two thousand* dollars."

Liam's gaze flew to hers and found her eyebrows raised, a small smile on her face. "Oh, well, Rose—it was planned for her to bid on me. That's all." He couldn't help feeling flattered though. "Good cause and all that."

"Yeah, those Everett sisters have a lot of money to spare."

"I wouldn't know," Liam said coolly. What was Pearl saying? He had money to spare too, but he was still working for funding and grants for the clinic.

"Have you asked them if they'd like to make a donation to the hospital renovation?"

Liam blinked, completely blindsided by the question. "I haven't," he said as diplomatically as possible.

"Well, consider it," she said. "They must have billions of dollars from their twenty-year career. The Whittakers too. I know their bank accounts all have nine zeroes."

"How would you know that?" Liam asked, narrowing his eyes at Pearl.

"I can search the Internet," she said. "They own and operate one of the biggest energy companies in the country. Their estimated net worth is astronomical."

"Well, it's just an estimate," Liam said, wondering if he'd find himself or his family with an Internet search about estimated net worth.

"And you know them, right?"

"I mean, I've met a few of them."

Pearl cocked her head, missing nothing. "I'd like you to ask them to make a donation."

"Why can't you do it?" he asked, feeling a bit like he was trying to skate on thin ice without blades.

"Because you have the…*personal* connection." She gave him a knowing look, like she knew he'd kissed Rose at the lodge and never wanted to kiss another woman again. Only her. Always her.

Pearl gave him a grin that felt a bit wolfish and left him standing there as she walked away.

He sighed and turned back to the laptop. If he could secure the top tier of the grant, maybe he could justify not mentioning a donation to Rose and her sisters, or any of the Whittakers.

By the time he finished and remembered that Rose had texted, another couple of hours had gone by. He cursed himself as he looked at her texts and saw that she'd asked him about the great news.

Asked him if he had time for dinner, and that she was down in the valley at her sister's.

Asked him if he'd always be working nights and weekends.

A throbbing pain started behind his eyes. He wanted to tell her everything, go to dinner with her, cuddle on those comfy couches in the basement of the lodge. Wanted to go home to her on nights and weekends.

It was only six-thirty, and surely they had time for dinner. So he called her, because he hadn't heard her voice for a couple of days, and he was in agony over it.

"Hey," she said, her voice half soft and half hard.

Everything inside him sighed. "Hey."

"You never answered my texts."

"The hospital administrator came by right when you texted."

"It was hours ago."

Just a couple, and Liam frowned. "I had some things to take care of."

"You always do."

"Rose," he said. "I'd love to go to dinner."

"I can't," she said. "I'm already back up at the lodge, and Beau says it's going to snow again."

"Please," he whispered, rubbing his fingers across the bridge of his nose. He needed some painkillers. "I'll grab something on the way up to my place, and you can drive down and meet me. I'm on Prospect Lake."

Silence came through the line, and Liam knew she was considering it. "Or I'll come up and get you and we can go back to my place. I don't have one of those fancy theater rooms, but we can curl up by the fire. I'll get whatever you want to eat." He took a deep breath. "Please, Rose."

"Fine." She sighed. "Give me the address."

He did, and she said, "And I'm feeling like Chinese tonight. Extra egg rolls, please. And some of those pork potstickers."

"Done," he said. "See you in about an hour?"

"I'll be there."

The call ended, and Liam stood up, leaving the clipboard right where it was. As he walked out, he wondered if he should hand the clinic over to someone else. But the thought felt poisonous in his soul, and he just couldn't do it.

An hour later, he had all the food set out on the counter. The fire in the gas unit was on high. And Rose still hadn't arrived.

It had not started snowing, and Liam thought for once the predictions would be wrong.

After another fifteen minutes of waiting, and with his stomach demanding some of that food that was just sitting there, Liam moved to the front windows. He saw a truck sitting in his driveway, but no one had come to the door.

He opened the front door and stepped outside. Rose made him come all the way down the steps and the sidewalk before she got out of the truck. "What are you doing out here?" he asked. "It's freezing."

"I was trying to decide if I should come in or not." She looked at him openly, pure vulnerability in her eyes.

"Why is that such a hard decision?" Liam asked, ice moving through his veins, and not just because of the sub-arctic temperatures. He couldn't lose Rose. She was the best thing in his life, and he hadn't even known he needed her.

She shrugged. "I feel like maybe I'll always be second to the clinic."

"That's not true," he said. "I just have a lot going on right now."

"You said you had good news."

"I do, and it just took some of my time today." He extended his hand toward her. "Please come in."

She put her hand in his, and Liam's heart celebrated. He led her into the house, and barely had the door closed before he pressed her against it and said, "I missed you so much." In the next moment, his mouth found hers and kissed her. Kissed her with everything he had so she wouldn't doubt him. So she wouldn't have to make such hard decisions about whether she should come in or not.

"Liam," she breathed into his mouth, and then she kissed him again.

Okay, so at least she missed him too.

CHAPTER 15

A month passed, and the snow stayed. But as April disappeared into May, the sun finally started to unearth the land beneath the drifts.

Her life had been divided into two parts—one with Liam in it and one where he wasn't. Her parents had come in late February, and they'd both stayed for a week. Then her father had gone back to Nashville to finish up some things before he retired, and her mother had stayed.

She lived in the room next door to Rose—at least for one more night. Rose had purchased a house in town, in one of the newer neighborhoods that had sprung up in the last year, and moving day was tomorrow.

She didn't have a whole lot at the lodge except for clothes and toiletries. No furniture. No kitchen things. But she had hired a moving company and spent many long hours on the phone with them for what to pack and what to leave. Her dad was going to go through everything that was left and either donate it, trash it, or sell it.

In fact, most of that had already been done, as the movers had left Tennessee six days ago. The truck would be here tomorrow morning, right on schedule, as she'd just gotten off the phone with Jeff, the driver who'd been communicating with her for a few weeks now.

She entered the kitchen to find Beau so he could mobilize the men he knew. All of the Whittaker brothers that lived in Coral Canyon would be there, and Beau claimed he could get several more big, strong cowboys from church to help.

"Hey," she said to the man standing in the kitchen. But it wasn't Beau. He turned toward her, and he was clearly a Whittaker. Andrew, then. She hadn't seen much of him or his wife, as they lived in town, and Andrew was purportedly the busiest Whittaker because he still had a more-than-full time job at the energy company.

"Hey, Rose," he said with a grin. "Coffee?"

"I'm good, thanks." She sat at the bar and flipped her phone over, a bit out of place with this Whittaker brother. Graham didn't make an appearance at the lodge every day, but he and Laney and their kids came every Sunday, or Beau and Lily and Rose went down to their ranch. Andrew and Becca had come for Sunday dinner a few times, but Rose had never been one-on-one with him.

"How's Chrissy?" Rose asked, reaching deep into her memory for the name of Andrew's daughter. "Wasn't she sick a couple of weeks ago?"

"Yes," he said, a smile crossing his face. "Thank you for remembering. She's doing a lot better, thanks."

"Did you figure out what was wrong with her?"

"Chicken pox," he said, lifting his mug to his lips. "So we were in complete quarantine for a while. Your boyfriend was quite helpful."

"Oh, you saw Liam?"

"He came to the house a couple of times."

Rose smiled and nodded like she'd known all along. But of course she didn't. Rose was not part of Liam's work life at all, a fact she'd been continually brushing away all spring.

"I'm available to help you move tomorrow," Andrew said. "I have a big favor in return."

"All right," she said, hoping she'd be able to say yes. She couldn't expect him to give up his day schlepping her boxes and not help him if she could.

"It's non-obligatory," he said. "You can say no, and I'll still gladly come help you move."

"All right," she said again. "What is it?"

"My wife hasn't been out of the house in a while, and I think she's going stir-crazy." The more he spoke, the faster he got. "I want to take her out of town for a few days, but I need a babysitter for our almost-two-year-old. Beau says you're great with baby Charlie, and—"

"Yes," Rose said with a smile.

Andrew blinked at her. "Really?"

"Really. I love kids."

Andrew chuckled and came around the counter, gripped her head, and placed a kiss on the very top of it. "Thank you, Rose. Thank you. I'll get all the details worked out and let you know."

And that was how Rose became a babysitter when she'd used to be a country music superstar. And she didn't mind one little bit.

———

THE FOLLOWING MORNING, ROSE WOKE IN THE ROOM WHERE SHE'D been living for the past few months and took a deep breath. "This is it," she told herself.

She'd made it out of bed and into a pair of jeans and a T-shirt with a suitcase on the front before she heard a *bang!* and Vi call, "Hello?"

Rose moved toward the door, and had barely made it down the hall when Vi called again. "What?" she said over the railing, still moving to get down the stairs. Because something was going on.

Vi had tears running down her face, and a smile so wide, that only one thing could've happened. "Todd asked you to marry him," Rose said, practically tripping over her feet as she ran down the stairs. *Don't fall, don't fall*, she coached herself.

She reached the bottom of the stairs, and Vi had her hand out for Rose to see the diamond. "Oh, my goodness." She could barely breathe at the sight of it. "Vi, oh, Vi, it's beautiful." She grabbed onto her sister and hugged her, jealous and joyful all at the same time. "I'm so happy for you."

"What's going on?" Lily asked, and Vi spun toward her.

"Todd finally asked me to marry him." She rushed through the living room, Rose right behind her. Rose took Charlie so Lily could shriek and bounce up and down as she celebrated with Vi.

Finally, Vi took a deep breath and said, "Do you think I can plan a wedding by Christmas?"

"Of course," Lily said immediately. "It's barely June."

"Mom and Dad will be here anyway," Vi said, following Lily into the kitchen, both of them apparently forgetting that Rose stood there with Charlie. Such actions would've bothered her in the past, but she was determined not to be upset today.

It was her moving day, the start of a new life for her. And besides, she wasn't the last one to know, because her mom came downstairs and said, "What's going on? Was Vi yelling?"

Rose handed her Charlie and said, "Yep. Come on, Mom. You've got to see this ring." She stood back and watched the women in her family interact, realizing how blessed she was. Then she joined the fray and made toast for everyone, accepted coffee from Lily, who made a delicious brew, and laughed with everyone in the kitchen.

Soon enough, it was time for her to finish packing her bag and get down to the house she'd bought. She bypassed Prospect Lake Road, almost desperate to see Liam before she moved in. The clinic was seven days from opening, and she didn't expect to see him for more than a few hours this morning until that was done.

She'd said it was okay, but she was getting tired of living two lives. He'd promised her that his life wouldn't be so crazy once the clinic opened, and she'd been living on that promise and a prayer for weeks now.

She pulled up to the two-story house on the north side of town, her backyard bordering the Wyoming wilds beyond, to find Liam's LandRover already there. The moving truck was too, and as she got out, she caught sight of him coming out of the open front door.

"There you are," he said with a smile. He swept his arms around her and kissed her. "They got here five minutes ago. I let them in."

"Thank you." She took a deep breath, getting mostly the spicy scent of his cologne and a little bit of fresh air. "Today's the day. You're still coming for dinner, right?"

"Wouldn't miss it. You'll be at the grand opening next Monday, right?"

Rose gazed up at him, thinking of Vi's new diamond and wondering if Liam would ever buy her one. They'd talked about kids, but he'd honestly never said if he was okay having kids he'd never wanted. He'd told her more about his life before they'd met, and Rose was honestly happy with their relationship.

Sometimes spending time with him felt like a negotiation, and she didn't like that. But she'd seen Lily and Beau do the same thing, and in some of her late-night chats with her mom over the past few months had revealed the same thing.

So maybe Rose wasn't great at negotiating for what she wanted. Maybe she'd always been given exactly what she wanted. She didn't like feeling spoiled and selfish, so she'd been working really hard to accept when Liam could spend his time with her and when he needed to be at the clinic.

"I wouldn't miss it," she said. "I even found the prettiest dress to wear. It's pink."

"Ooh, pink." He pressed his lips to her temple again as Beau and Graham arrived. "Good thing you brought the big guns," he said, glancing toward the semi truck. "I had no idea a single woman could have so much stuff."

Rose rolled her eyes and gently pushed him away from her. "Go get another box, doctor." She looked up at him. "Oops, you're a cowboy today."

He grinned, tipped that sexy cowboy hat at her, and walked over to the Whittaker brothers. They all started taking boxes inside. Rose didn't relish the idea of unpacking them, but at least the movers had followed her directions and labeled each one in large, black letters for where it went.

She'd come down to the house yesterday and put small signs on the doorframes so the boxes would get where they needed to go. Andrew and Becca pulled up, and Rose took a detour over to their car.

"Hey," she said to them. Becca hugged her, which sent surprise through her, while Andrew bent to get their daughter out of the car. He held her on his hip, and wow, Rose had seen Beau handle tiny Charlie, but to see another tall, burly man wearing a cowboy hat and handling a little girl with such love sent hope right through Rose's heart.

She glanced over her shoulder to see if Liam was around. She couldn't see him.

"This is Chrissy," Andrew said. "Chrissy, this is Rose."

"Hey, baby," Rose said, and Chrissy just stared at her blankly.

"She takes a bit to warm up to people," Becca said, taking her and setting her on the ground. "We're going to help Rose move into this house today, sweetie. Let's go." The toddler waddled along beside Becca, both of them moving very slow. Andrew walked ahead and picked up a box, glancing over at them before he headed to the house.

Rose caught sight of Liam as he came out, and they met at the back of the semi. He grinned at her and picked up another box, not even glancing at Chrissy.

"Do you know Becca?" Rose asked before he could walk away. "And her daughter, Chrissy?"

"Oh, Andrew's wife." He put his box down. "Sure, hello."

"My boyfriend, Liam."

Becca shook his hand and Rose handed her a small toy. "Look, baby. You take this."

Liam looked at Chrissy and then back to Rose. She scooped the girl up into her arms and said, "Let's see if we can beat the buff cowboy to the house." She took off toward the front door, jogging as best as she could with the child in her arms. She giggled, and Rose laughed, and she heard Andrew chuckling behind her too.

"Oh, we're going to beat him. Don't let him pass us, Chrissy." Rose went up the steps to the door and paused, exaggerating her breathing. "We did it." She looked at the little girl, who was smiling and gripping her apple squishy for all she was worth.

"You guys cheated," he said from behind them.

Rose faced him. "We did not. You're just slow."

His eyebrows lifted, and she moved to the side to let him in so he could take his box into the kitchen. Their eyes locked and didn't let go until he passed her completely. Rose felt like someone had stuffed the sun into her chest and turned it on high.

"Come on," she said to Chrissy. "Don't let him tell you we cheated." Rose felt a bit out of breath, as she didn't really spend a whole lot of time in the gym. Certainly not the way Vi did. She found her sister in the backyard with Jetstream, and Rose put Chrissy down on the lawn. The dog came over, and she started laughing as he licked her face.

"Jet, stop it." Vi pushed the dog away, and Chrissy reached for him again. Rose watched them both, her heart expanding with love for the simplest of interactions and the simplest of creatures.

"Rose," someone called, and she stood.

"You're okay with them?" she asked.

"Yeah, go."

As Rose walked into the house, Becca came out, both of them smiling.

"Your dad just got here," she said, and Rose thanked her.

Not only was her father there, but at least a dozen more men from church, and they all looked like they could haul tall buildings with a single bicep.

"We want to know where you want this couch," her dad said, and Rose put on her bossy pants. Maybe moving day wouldn't be so bad, and as long as she had a bed to sleep in that night, she could deal with anything else.

Liam kissed her goodbye when he had to leave for his final meeting at the hospital, and Rose focused on getting all the pieces of her new life in line. Right where she wanted them.

Once everything was off the truck and in the right place in the house, everyone left.

Except Rose. She stood in her new living room and realized there was still one piece missing.

Someone to share this new life with, and she was really beginning to wonder if that man was Liam, or if she was once again wasting her time with the wrong man.

CHAPTER 16

L iam worked so much, he slept better than he had in months. He'd never slept particularly well overseas, but that life seemed so far from this new one in Coral Canyon. He couldn't believe he'd been here for almost six months now. Couldn't believe the clinic he'd envisioned was going to actually open.

One week, he thought as he pulled into the parking lot and got out of his LandRover. Things were going well at Rose's, so while he wished he could be there with her, he also knew she was in good hands.

He'd met her parents months ago when they'd come to visit, and her mother had been living here since then. He liked her mom and dad, and they seemed to like him. They were so different from his parents, though they'd basically raised and managed the Everett Sisters through over two decades of a very successful career.

They didn't seem pretentious or stuffy the way his parents did, and he tried to shove the worry about having them here for the grand opening back into the hole where he'd been keeping it.

His anxiety increased with each day toward the opening, toward the day his parents and Lars would come stay in the summer cabin with him. He needed to follow Rose's lead and find a house of his own, but he simply hadn't had time.

After the opening. Liam had been living his life with those three words constantly in the back of his mind. He'd make sure Rose knew how much he wanted to be with her—after the opening. He'd find a house—after the opening. He'd get out and explore the wonders of nature in Coral Canyon—after the opening. He'd get to church on a more regular basis—after the opening.

He pushed into the clinic to find it hopping with people. Happiness and hope hit him right in the chest, especially when Arthur approached him and shook his hand.

"You made it," Liam said. "How'd everything go with the move?"

"Great." The doctor had been scheduled to move in over the weekend, and he'd insisted to Liam that he didn't need help. "Kami is at the lake with the girls today. Just got a text that they're loving it."

"I'm glad," Liam said, and he was. If he could keep his doctors and nurses happy, they'd stay, work hard, and the clinic would be successful.

Paul waved at him, and Liam said, "Excuse me," to go see what mishap had happened now. But for probably the first time, it wasn't bad news.

"Final inspection," Paul said. "Let's go over it." He carried a clipboard with a ton of paper attached to it, and started walking around the clinic, showing Liam every little thing. Light switches, water shut offs, hot water heater, furnace, air conditioner, overhead ducts, internal vacuums, storage areas, all of it.

"And we passed?" Liam asked.

Paul signed his name on one paper, then another. "All passed." He handed the pages to Liam. "You're set to open, doctor."

Relief spread through Liam with the speed of light, and he

shook Paul's hand and watched the construction manager walk out of the clinic, hopefully for the last time.

Now, they just needed to get all their staff meetings done, their schedules, get all the rooms stocked and supplied, and meet with Pearl to finalize the plans on the grand opening. Liam took a big breath and told himself he could do it.

He'd come this far, and he could finish. He could.

Hours later, their first staff meeting was almost over when the rain started. Since it was early June, the weather was still unpredictable and could change in a matter of minutes. Liam watched it splash the windows outside the break room where they'd been sitting for a while now. Dr. Gurnsey was almost finished, and Liam hoped he could get right out so he wouldn't be late to Rose's dinner.

She'd planned no housewarming party. Only what she called "a simple dinner" just for the two of them. He couldn't be late. Couldn't miss it.

When the first drops of rain landed on the table in front of him, he knew he was not going to Rose's that night. His heart sank as he jumped to his feet, pure panic rushing through his body.

"The roof is leaking," he blurted, something he probably should've kept to himself, especially with Pearl in the room.

The presentation stopped, and everyone seemed to zero in on the water slowly but steadily dripping from the ceiling tiles.

"I'll call Paul," he said, fumbling for his phone at the same time Pearl said, "I thought we passed the physical inspection."

"We did," Liam said darkly as the line rang. Pearl frowned at him as if Liam had climbed up on the roof and deliberately sabotaged it. Didn't she understand he wanted this clinic to open as badly as she did?

He was so, so tired, and Paul sounded the same when Liam told him there was water dripping into the break room. "Check everywhere else," he said. "I'll be there in twenty minutes."

So Liam instructed everyone to spread out and see if there

were any more leaks in the clinic. They all reported back to the main nurse's station with negative reports. So just one small leak. He could deal with it.

He sent everyone home, and he and Pearl waited for Paul. He showed up and started using his fancy gadgets to detect moisture behind walls ceilings. "Yep, there's a leak there. Let me see where it's coming from."

He got out a ladder and Liam stepped away to call Rose.

She answered with, "Tell me you're still coming."

"I am," he said, hoping he wasn't going to be a liar too. "There's a small leak in the roof we discovered when it started raining, and I'm—I have to stay for a little longer."

She sighed and said nothing. Liam didn't blame her. She'd been living her life with the same words he had. *After the opening.*

"Get here when you can," she said, and then she added, "See you soon."

He sighed and turned back to the clinic. It felt eerie when it was empty, and a flash of pride at what he'd done here stole through him. Hopefully, Rose would be able to see the value of what she'd sacrificed for this clinic. What he had.

Half an hour later, Paul came down out of the crawl space and said, "The leak is not in the roof. It's coming from the main part of the hospital."

All Liam heard was *not in the roof.* Paul started talking to Pearl about rerouting the rain gutters that came off that corner of the hospital, and how they needed to be adjusted so they didn't leak into the crawl space.

Liam wanted to go, because this obviously wasn't a flaw with his clinic. But he didn't dare, not until Pearl said he could. Why, he wasn't sure. She really wasn't his boss.

But he stayed while Paul set up fans to dry out the crawl space and made a temporary fix until he could get his welder out once the rain stopped to get the gutters where they needed to go.

Finally, Paul left, and Liam didn't have a reason to stay either.

But at that point, he was two hours late getting to Rose's, and he didn't want to waste any more time going home to shower.

He showed up on her doorstep smelling like bleach and antiseptic, a measure of desperation and panic pulling through him.

"I'm so sorry," he said when she opened the door. He stepped inside, the house completely different than it had been that afternoon. "Look at this place." He moved his gaze from the spacious living room, which was somehow put together perfectly, to the woman beside him.

She wore a pair of jeans and a sweatshirt that hung off one shoulder. "Look at you." He smiled and let his gaze linger on the bare skin of her upper arm. "I'm sorry," he said again.

"I know you are." She hugged him, and he felt himself falling all the way in love with her.

"I'm trying," he said. "I've never had to do so much before."

"I kept dinner warm." She went into the kitchen first, and he followed her, wondering if she was still frustrated or angry with him. She didn't seem to be, but she wasn't really participating in the conversation the way he'd like.

She pulled a huge Dutch oven out of the oven and grunted as she set it on the stovetop. "I made pot roast."

"There's not chocolate in there, is there?" he asked, hoping that would break the remaining ice surrounding her.

She rolled her eyes and smiled. "No. No chocolate."

He picked up one of the plates she'd laid on the counter. "Are you mad at me?"

"Yes," she said, facing him and looking right at him. She'd always been so good at articulating how she felt. "But then I decided it wasn't worth being mad about. I thought about this man I dated once. Cole Kingston. I met him in Nashville while my sisters and I were between albums. Once we started on the next one, with all the writing and then the recording and then the touring, well, I didn't see him very much."

She picked up a plate too and removed the lid from the Dutch oven. The most delicious smell of beef and onions filled the air. "I kept explaining to him that this was my job. I couldn't just not tour with my sisters. He broke up with me."

Liam's heart stuttered and skipped. "So is that what you're going to do?" He stepped to her side in front of the stove. "Break up with me?"

She looked up at him, her eyes soft and so blue he wanted to dive into them and stay forever. In that moment, he realized he was in love with her. He bent down and she tilted up, and this kiss felt a bit different than any of their others.

He'd kissed her in a slow, passionate way while they were supposed to be watching a movie. He'd kissed her with need and almost a frantic quality when he hadn't seen her for a while. He'd kissed her quickly before he headed to work, and for a longer time when she had to go back up to the lodge.

But he'd never kissed her with this hint of forgiveness in her touch, and when she ducked her head and broke their connection, Liam felt like the luckiest man on Earth to have found this good woman.

Now, he just had to figure out how to keep her in his life by making sure she was happy. *He* had to make her happy.

———

A WEEK LATER, LIAM PACED IN THE KITCHEN OF THE SUMMER CABIN, expecting his parents and brother to arrive at any moment. Sure enough, he heard a car door slam from outside, and he quickly crossed through the house to the front door so he could greet them.

The grand opening would happen the following morning, and they were meeting Rose that night for the first time too. Liam should've known better than to pack so many important things into less than fifteen hours, but apparently, he enjoyed the feeling of nearly failing a little too much.

"Mom," he said as she came up the sidewalk wearing a long black skirt with a white and green checkered blouse. He went down the steps to give her a quick hug. He shook his father's hand and then Lars', and gestured back up the steps as if they needed his permission to enter their own house.

"All ready for tomorrow?" his dad asked.

"Yep," he said. "Yes, all ready." Every piece had been checked and double-checked, from the Mayor's schedule to the food to the staff bios and who would do the introductions. "How's the real estate business? Going into summer is good, right?"

Lars took over, detailing all these houses they had for sale, and how he'd closed on a mountain deal last week. The pride in his voice made Liam want to punch him, but he kept nodding and smiling.

His phone crackled, and he practically lunged for it. But he didn't have much hope that she'd like his family any more than he did. She would, however, probably be much better at pretending to.

"Rose is here." He faced his parents and brother. "Let's be nice to her, okay?"

"We're nice," his mom said as if she'd never looked down her nose at anyone before.

"I really like this woman," Liam said, something he'd never actually said or thought before. He turned toward the door, expecting them to come with him and unsurprised when they did.

So Rose met them all on the front porch, and Liam introduced her to his mom and dad, and then Lars. She shook hands with a perfect smile on her face, and his mom gave her two air kisses, one on each cheek.

"So lovely to meet you," she said, holding onto Rose's shoulders. "You look so familiar, dear." She glanced at Liam.

"She's one of the Everett Sisters," he said, unsure if his high-society family would know the country music group.

His mother's eyes widened, and she sucked in a breath. "Of course," she said, still so dignified. "Rose Everett."

Liam refrained from rolling his eyes. His mother didn't know

Rose Everett from any of the members of her bridge club. But at least she was being nice, and she asked Rose how she was liking her new house as they went back into the cabin.

Liam breathed deeply, and he was once again impressed with Rose as she engaged with each member of his family like she'd been waiting her whole life to meet them.

By the time dinner was over, and he could escape with her alone, he was ready for his family to be gone. He held Rose's hand as they walked along the shore of the lake, and he said, "You're brilliant, you know that?"

She laughed and clutched his hand with both of hers. "Because I can make small talk and act interested in people?"

"Exactly." He pressed his lips to her temple and said, "Rose, I think I'm falling in love with you."

She stilled and turned toward him. "Liam." She shook her head. "You can't say those things to me unless they're true."

"Of course they're true," he said, his eyes searching hers and wondering why she looked like she was about to cry.

She didn't say she loved him too. But when she kissed him, he felt it in her touch, in the urgent way she pressed into him but kissed him in a whole, round way.

And he was definitely all the way in love with her. Now, if he could just make it through the grand opening of the clinic in the morning, he could finally put his focus where it belonged: On Rose Everett.

CHAPTER 17

Rose thought she might be more nervous than Liam, and she kept slicking her palms down the front of her pink, frilly dress. She stood to the side with Liam's parents, in the front but not the center.

It seemed like the whole town had shown up for the official grand opening and ribbon cutting ceremony for the new emergency clinic. Liam stood with the Mayor, talking as if he didn't have a care in the world.

But Rose had been with him only a few minutes ago, and he'd been as nervous as a cat in room full of rocking chairs. Then he'd put on a mask and stepped through the doors. She marveled watching him, as he seemed to move from role to role effortlessly.

Nine o'clock came, and he handed the Mayor an overly large pair of scissors, took a mic from a woman who looked like she belonged behind the desk of a Fortune 500 company, and stepped to a spot right behind the huge, red bow in the middle of the ribbon.

"Welcome, everyone," he said, the speakers throwing his voice out into the crowd. He gave them a moment to quiet down. "I'm so pleased to be here with all of you today, for this opening of the emergency clinic. Just because it's called Coral Canyon Afterhours Clinic doesn't mean you can't come in the middle of the day. It simply means we're here for you when you need us."

Rose loved the deep, rolling sound of his voice, and she thought of his words from last night as they'd strolled along the lakeshore.

I think I'm falling in love with you.

They still made her warm all these hours later, as if the June sunshine wasn't doing a good enough job.

"So without further ado, we've brought in Mayor Berry to do the honors of opening us up right." He indicated that the Mayor should come forward.

He wore a smile the size of the Gulf of Mexico and cut the giant ribbon, which fell in two pieces to cheers and applause.

"And we're open!" Liam said into the mic before handing it back to the stuffy woman in the administrative skirt suit. Rose watched her for a moment, then her attention was stolen by Liam as he took her hand and squeezed it almost painfully.

She went with him into the clinic, where the public was pouring in to be able to see the facilities before they truly became operational. Liam had thought of everything, and he and his staff positioned themselves in different locations to answer questions.

Two hours later, the main event was over. The clinic was open for real, and the public had dispersed back to their homes, families, and jobs.

"You did it," Rose said, her pinky toe on her right foot screaming at her to find a different pair of shoes quickly.

Liam stood in the middle of the waiting room in the lobby and looked around. "I did it." His gaze landed on her, and he kissed her standing right there for everyone to see.

Rose didn't care. She wanted to be wherever he was, and she thought she might be falling in love with him too.

———

"We'll be fine," she said to Andrew and Becca, both of whom wore almost identical expressions of concern and worry. She bounced their toddler on her hip. "Right, Chrissy? Wave bye-bye to Mommy and Daddy."

Rose flapped her fingers, and Chrissy did too, which made her smile. "Seriously. You guys go on. We'll be fine."

She was staying at their house to make it easier for Chrissy, have all of the supplies and food she needed, and she planned to have a great three-day weekend with the two-year-old. After all, Liam had to work this weekend, so her other option was to sit in her new house by herself or go up to the lodge and listen to Vi, Lily, and her mother plan a Christmas wedding for her sister.

Andrew and Becca left, and Rose went back inside with Chrissy. "All right, baby," she said. "What should we do first?"

Chrissy picked up the handle to a toy vacuum and began pushing it around the room. Otto, the giant yellow lab of the household, came over and sniffed Rose like she might be made of something delicious he wanted to lick. In the end, he deemed her human and flopped onto the floor to take a nap.

The little girl made vacuum noises with her mouth and ran the toy into Otto a few times before he got up and moved over a few feet, re-flopping down and starting to snore a moment later. Rose enjoyed the normalcy of it.

She went over to the kitchen table, where Becca said she'd left a few notes. A booklet was more like it, and Rose flipped through a few pages to read about how to feed and water the strays in the backyard, and all about Chrissy's sleeping and eating schedule.

Mothering and caring for children came naturally to Rose, so when it was time for lunch, she made macaroni and cheese and laughed when Chrissy tried to pick up the slippery noodles with her pudgy fingers. She gave her peach chunks according to Becca's instructions and put her down for a nap.

The days passed quickly until Andrew and Becca returned, and while Rose was sure Chrissy loved her and that they'd had fun taking Otto to the park, and going out on the lake with Beau and Lily and baby Charlie, and cuddling on the couch reading books, Chrissy sure was happy to see her mom and dad again.

Rose loved the small-town life, and she wandered through the Summerfest booths with her sisters and her mom, buying wood signs and letterboards for her house. She sipped sweet tea her momma made on the front steps of the lodge and called someone to come install a hammock in one of the big trees in her backyard.

She felt like she was marking time. Living, but not really alive. The summer slipped away from her, and she felt like she often had on tour. Like a ghost everyone screamed for but that no one actually wanted to keep.

Once, when she'd been in therapy, she'd identified this feeling as loneliness, and it came even when she was surrounded by people.

And she realized that her life in Coral Canyon was no different than the one she'd had in Nashville. The house wasn't as big. The work wasn't the same. The mountains were bigger.

But she was still Rose Everett, baby sister to Vi and Lily, who talked about the wedding constantly and never asked for her opinion. Rose Everett, the woman who desperately wanted a family but ended up babysitting for her sister, and her sister's brother-in-laws instead of moving toward having kids of her own.

Rose Everett, singer and songwriter who wrote sad ballads, and the one she was working on now was about a woman who couldn't get her boyfriend to leave work in time to get home for dinner.

It was so true to life that it made Rose sadder than she already was.

One day, about the time July turned into August, someone knocked on her front door. She opened it to find her mother standing there, a paper pastry bag in her hand. "Hello, Rose." She moved into the house with grace and elegance, the same way her mother had done everything for years.

"Mom," Rose said. "What are you doing here? I thought Vi was meeting with the cake artist this morning."

"She is. She doesn't need me." She moved into the kitchen and set the bag on the counter. "I brought some of those lemon poppy seed muffins I know you like."

They had huge sugar crystals on top, and Rose carefully peeled the top of the muffin off and took a bite. "Mm."

But there was more to this visit, and Rose knew it. Still, she let her mom take a few bites of her muffin and then pour herself a cup of coffee. "You don't seem very happy, dear," she said, finally looking straight at her.

Rose wanted to protest, but the truth was, she wasn't very happy. So she shrugged instead and took another bite of her muffin.

"Is it because of the wedding?"

"Partly," she said. "Lily and Vi have never involved me all that much." She tried not to let the hurt infuse her voice, but it did anyway. And her mother would've known even if it hadn't.

"They don't mean to."

"I know that." They were simply closer in age and better friends. Lily had been married in Coral Canyon and knew all the best professionals to hire. Rose knew it wasn't personal. It only felt that way.

"And what about Liam?" Her mother tucked her hair behind her ear and moved to stand behind her. She began braiding Rose's hair, and the gesture was so tender and so needed, that Rose's chest tightened.

"I don't know," she said. "He's so busy at work." Her throat narrowed too much to say anything else, and her mom finished braiding her hair in silence.

"Maybe you should say something to him. Tell him how much you miss him, that you love him, something."

"Daddy worked a lot," Rose said. "How did you deal with that?"

Her mom let go of the end of the braid, and Rose felt it loosen. She sat beside Rose at the kitchen counter. "I was so busy with you girls, sometimes I didn't noticed that your father wasn't there. Then, when the group started, we both poured our energy into that. It was something we worked on together, so from then on, we were always together."

Rose nodded, pinched off another piece of muffin, and put it in her mouth. "Well, there's no way I can work at the clinic."

"Why not?"

Rose looked at her mom, realizing she was serious. "I don't have any medical skills."

"Surely Liam needs people to answer phones. Or send out bills. Or call insurance companies. Why can't you do that?"

Rose didn't have an answer for that question, and a new idea had been inserted into her mind. Maybe she should go to where Liam was. Wouldn't stealing a glimpse of him as he saw patients be better than pining for him while she swung in the hammock? Couldn't sneaking a kiss in his office be as thrilling as kissing him at his cabin?

"Just think about it," her mom said. "I don't like seeing you this way. Reminds me of that summer when you needed to see a counselor."

"I know," Rose said. "But I'm better than that, Mom. I am." And she was. She had some coping strategies for when she felt left out and forgotten. They might not be working, but she at least could recognize the feelings.

"All right, well, I'm taking Vi to Jackson Hole this afternoon for a dress fitting." She trailed her fingers across Rose's shoulders, something she'd done countless times before. Rose took a measure of her mother's peace and comfort before she left.

Then she got on the computer to see if there were any job openings at the clinic. It had only been open for two months, but she whispered a plea to the Lord as she typed in a search term.

"Please, Lord," she said. "I need to know if this thing with Liam is real or not. Let there be a job for me at the clinic."

CHAPTER 18

"Your girlfriend just applied for a job."

Liam turned from the pile of folders on his desk—the files he had to go through for the patients they'd seen yesterday. "I'm sorry?" He blinked at Susan, the office manager for the clinic.

"Aren't you dating Rose Everett?"

"Yes." His head hurt. In fact, everything on Liam's body hurt. He thought he was definitely coming down with something, especially now that the weather had started to cool again. They'd seen an uptick in the number of people coming in with strep throat and sinus infections, and he felt like he had the inklings of both.

"She just applied to be an evening filer."

The words made no sense. "She doesn't need a job."

"Yeah, well, neither do you." Susan gave him a friendly smile. "Do you want me to interview her or not? We do need someone." She looked at the files on his desk. "Case in point."

"Let me talk to her," he said, his thoughts going in all directions. Susan left his office, and Liam closed the door behind her before pulling out his phone to call Rose.

"Hey," she said. "Are you almost done there?"

If he had an evening filer, he would be. "Rose," he said. "I just heard you applied for a job here."

"Yes," she said.

"Why?"

"Because Liam," she said, and he could hear the frustration in those two words. "*You're* there."

He expected more than that, but she didn't give him anything else. The only other romances he'd had were with co-workers, and he wasn't sure he wanted to have to establish lines at the clinic.

"You don't need the money, do you?" he asked.

"You're so dim," she said. "I mean, for a smart guy, you're just so out to lunch. *I miss you.*"

Liam took a few moments to absorb the power in her words. "So you thought if you got a job filing in the evenings, we could spend more time together."

She said nothing, a silent confirmation. Finally, she said, "You promised me you'd have more time for us once the clinic opened." Her voice sounded dangerously high and so, so far away.

Liam had no idea what to say. He knew what he'd promised her. He could work less. The truth was, he enjoyed his work. He thrived on the atmosphere in the clinic, especially when it was busy. He found his self-worth in helping others.

"I know," he said. Nothing more. He didn't know what to do.

"This isn't going to change, is it?" she asked. "Let me rephrase that. *You're* not going to change."

Liam ground his teeth together. "Can we talk about this later?"

"Sure," she said. "When you find a spare minute, come on by."

"Rose," he said, almost begging her to stay on the line.

"I changed my mind," she said. "I don't want the job."

"I'm quite happy to give you the job, if that's what you want." Someone knocked on his door, and Dr. Gurnsey poked his head in. When he saw Liam on the phone, he held up one hand and backed out of the office.

Liam really liked working with Arthur, and he tried to schedule himself with the other GP as often as possible. With four doctors on staff, no, Liam didn't have to work as much as he did.

Or at all. He could hire someone else and let his clinic run itself. He had an office manager. He had a maintenance team lead. He had a head nurse. They didn't need him.

No one *needed* him.

"I have to go," Rose said. "Good-bye, Liam." The line went dead, and he wondered if she'd just broken up with him. He was still reeling from the realization that he didn't feel needed. Not here. Not at the summer cabin. Nowhere.

Why was that? He'd done a great thing here in Coral Canyon. He'd done good work with Doctors Without Borders. But the fact was, he'd left, and the operation hadn't fallen apart. Of course it wouldn't. They'd just hire another doctor, send someone else to Nigeria, and he realized how utterly replaceable he was.

Here, there—and with Rose.

He opened the door, not sure what to do with his feelings or about Rose. "Arthur?" he asked. The man turned from where he'd been standing down the hall.

"Some of us are going to get wings after the shift change," he said. "You want to come?"

Liam did. But it was his night with Rose. Or maybe he didn't have that opportunity anymore. He wasn't sure of a whole lot.

"I think I'll pass," he said. "Thanks for inviting me though."

Arthur smiled and headed back out onto the patient floor. Liam returned to his office, shut the door, and leaned against it with a sigh. He needed to figure out what he wanted, and fast, before he lost something he couldn't get back.

An hour later, he stood on Rose's doorstep with a dozen

flowers that bore her namesake. When she opened the door, she took his breath away, same as she always did.

"I don't know why I pick the clinic over you," he said, thrusting the flowers toward her. "I'm sorry, Rose."

She took the bouquet and stepped back to let him in. He had the distinct thought that there would come a time when an apology would not be enough for her. An *I'm Sorry* would not heal the hurt he'd caused her.

"What do I need to do?" he asked her.

She shrugged and continued into the kitchen, where she got out a glass vase and filled it with water. The tension between them was as thick in person as it had been on the phone. And Liam had no idea how to break it.

Rose arranged the blooms and returned to the living room. She stood behind the couch and faced him. "Liam, who would you invite to our wedding?"

He opened his mouth to speak, but the question had blind-sided him. "I—what are you saying?"

"I'm asking who you'd invite to our wedding," she said, a little slower this time. "You know, people get married when they love each other, and you said months ago that you were falling in love with me." Her blue eyes stormed, and he noticed that her hair had new streaks in it. Darker ones. Some red. He liked them.

"So I'm asking who you'd invite to our wedding, if we were to get married."

"I...don't know. My parents. Lars."

"Three people." She started nodding, and Liam didn't like it. "This is the biggest event of your life. All of your friends and family should be there, cheering you on."

Liam felt hollow from head to toe. He wouldn't even want his parents there, though of course, he'd invite them. But surely his mother would find fault with something the cake artist had done, and probably the only reason Lars and his father would come was so they could buy new suits.

Rose smiled at him, but it wavered, and her lovely eyes filled with water. "And I don't even think you want your family there."

He shook his head, his jaw tight, his muscles tight, his heart so, so tight.

"And as far as I can tell, you don't have any friends here in Coral Canyon."

"That's not true," he said. "Arthur invited me for wings tonight."

Rose nodded again. "That's nice. But I think he's more of a co-worker than a real friend."

Had she not heard him? He'd never been invited to go out after work before. Of course, there wasn't anywhere to go in Columbia or Chad, and all the doctors slept in the same tent anyway, so technically, they always went home together.

"A friend is someone you trust," Rose said, taking one slow step laterally down the couch. "Someone you've told things you don't tell to anyone else. Someone who knows some of the worst things about you, and likes you anyway."

Well, when she put it like that, no, Liam didn't have any friends. "You're my friend," he said, his throat raw.

She took another step. "Yes, I am. And as your friend, I'm telling you that you need to quit at the clinic."

Quit the clinic? Liam gave a couple of short, barking laughs. "Oh, you're not kidding."

"No, I'm not."

"Rose, I'm a *doctor*."

"No, you're not."

"Yes, I am." A storm released in his chest, breaking through the tightness there. "It's all I've ever wanted to be; it's all I know how to be. It's *who* I am."

A tear splashed her cheek, and Liam hated it. Wanted to wipe it away and kiss her, tell her he'd do anything she wanted. But quit the clinic? That was insane.

Wasn't it?

"No," she said again, her voice tight and high and full of

emotion. "You're Liam Murphy, and being a doctor doesn't have anything to do with him."

"I have no idea what that means," he said, more anger in his tone than he meant to put there.

"I know." She gave short little nods. "I know you don't. That's the problem. You don't know who you are, or what you really want. So you've been chasing all over the world, looking for something—"

"No," he said.

"—that will give you worth," she finished.

"No," he said again, shaking his head this time. "You don't know that. You don't know me."

"But your worth doesn't come from what you do," she continued as if he hadn't even spoken. He hated those tears pouring down her face for a different reason now. She was trying to manipulate him, a tactic he was quite familiar with, thank you very much.

He clenched his jaw and looked away as she kept talking. "Your worth comes from who you *are*."

"I know who I am," he said, his voice edging up in volume. "I know who I am, Rose. I know what I've done, and you have no idea what it cost me to come here. No idea how I was treated before I left Switzerland. You met me on the plane, after—" He cut off, about to say something he'd regret.

But Rose had heard it. "After what?" she asked.

He looked away again, everything inside him swirling and blowing about, and he couldn't contain it anymore. "And I didn't deserve to be let go. I worked *so hard* for those people in Nigeria, and what happened was *not* my fault." He clenched his teeth again, but they just hurt. His heart ached. His head pounded. He hadn't told anyone that he'd left Doctors Without Borders unwillingly, not even his parents.

"So I can't quit the clinic," he said, very quietly. "I am a doctor, and no one is going to take that from me."

Rose lifted her chin, her eyes sparking with the same passion he felt coursing through him. "I wouldn't even try, Liam. But I can't be the doctor's wife, shut up in the summer cabin, all by myself. I can't. I won't. I shouldn't have to."

She'd never said she loved him, not in those three words. At the same time, that was exactly what she was saying when she talked about their wedding and being his wife.

"So that's it," he said.

"That, Liam, is up to you." She wiped her face slowly, deliberately, and left him standing in her living room. The sound of a door closing from down the hall met his ears, and Liam turned in a full circle, at a complete loss as to what to do now.

CHAPTER 19

Rose stayed in her house and cried for a few days. Then she pulled herself together, put on some warm clothes though it was still August, and drove up to Whiskey Mountain Lodge. Vi wanted to go to Jackson Hole and ride the gondola up to the top of the world.

She didn't want to miss it, though she knew her sisters and mother would take one look at her and demand to know what had happened. Would they really be shocked? Rose didn't think so. After all, Liam had made his choice obvious to everyone in town.

She'd been tempted to look up the story of his departure from Doctors Without Borders. Surely the Internet would have a story like that. But she respected him more than that, so she simply watched her video tutorials on how to do glimmer nails, slept more than she was awake, and made—and ate by herself— a batch of caramel popcorn every day.

So maybe putting on her best pair of jeans was a little uncomfortable. She'd put a baggy sweatshirt over them and no one would know. She meticulously applied her makeup, taking care to make her eyeshadow match the dusky browns in her shirt.

She hadn't been to the salon in a few weeks, but she

couldn't do anything about that now. She'd have to ride the gondola to the top of the Tetons with pink nails instead of a more earthy green that would've matched her outfit. To make up for it, she put a similar color of pink gloss on her lips, smacked them together, and deemed herself ready to face the public.

At the lodge, she found baby Charlie sitting up in a saucer, toys stuck to the outside as he flapped his hands at them. She giggled at him and crouched down when he grinned and waved both arms in excitement to see her.

"I know," she said. "I haven't seen you in so long. Look how big you're getting." She knew from the family text that he wasn't even on the charts for a baby his same age, but that the doctors were pleased with his growth for a preemie. "When's Grandpa coming, huh? And where's Mommy?"

"Right here," Lily said, and Rose glanced up to find her wiping her hands on a kitchen towel. "And Dad will be here in a couple of days. The house sold, and he packed it all up."

Rose stood and embraced Lily, her tears coming instantly. "It's so good to see you."

"Oh, okay." Lily clutched her and patted her back. "Rose, what's wrong?"

She couldn't answer, and thankfully Lily just held her tight, the way only the best big sister could.

"Is it Liam?"

Rose nodded, and Lily said, "Oh, sweetie, I'm so sorry."

"It's fine." Rose stepped back as abruptly as she'd grabbed onto her sister. She wiped her face, knowing she'd ruined fifteen minutes of work on her makeup. "I mean, he can't give up the clinic. But I guess he can give me up."

"I'm sure—"

"Lily," Vi called, appearing in the doorway that led out of the kitchen. "Where's—oh. What's going on?" She took another few tentative steps forward, her gaze solidly on Rose, who couldn't stop wiping her blasted face. "Don't tell me he broke up with you." She stopped a couple of feet away and put her hand on her hip.

"No," Rose said. "He didn't. I broke up with him." She sniffled, but she wouldn't break down again. "I think I've wasted enough time waiting, hoping, *praying* that he'll want to be with me."

Foolishness had never tasted so bitter before, and Rose had had a few instances where she'd made some idiotic decisions.

Vi exchanged a glance with Lily as Charlie started to fuss. Rose bent to attend to the baby, because she didn't want to deal with her sisters obvious friendship with each other. She knew they loved her. She did. She was friends with them too. But she couldn't help feeling like a third wheel around them.

"Maybe I'll just stay here with Charlie," she said, balancing him on her hip. He grabbed a fistful of her hair, and she carefully extracted it from his fingers.

"You can't do that," Vi said at the same time Lily said, "Beau's taking him down to his mother's."

Rose felt a sense of loss she didn't understand. "Oh, all right." She smiled at the baby, who didn't seem to notice that she'd been crying.

"I need your opinion," Vi said.

"You do not." Rose sent her a glare. "You and Mom and Lily have already planned everything, and you just invited me to go on the gondola with you." She never would've said such things under normal conditions. But she didn't feel like being very nice today.

"I'm sorry," she said quickly. "I'm not in a good mood. I should just go back home." But the thought of doing that made her throat close and her stomach twist. So maybe she could drive around a bit. Enjoy the fall leaves, as some of them had started to change already.

"No, you're coming." Vi stepped up to Rose and took Charlie from her. She handed the baby to Lily and then wrapped Rose in a hug. Rose didn't want to cry again, but she had so many emotions inside that she couldn't help it.

"I really miss you guys," she said. "And us writing songs, and working together, and touring, and all of it." She took a deep breath. "I mean, I get it. We're in a different stage of life now, and it's a good stage. I just feel…." Left out.

The truth was, Rose always felt left out. Left behind. Last.

"Less than," she finally said, pulling away and ducking her head. "Lily has Charlie now, and you're getting married, and what am I? Jobless, in a big house with nobody."

"Maybe you should do a solo album," Vi suggested. "People have always loved you more than me. I'm just the frumpy middle sister."

Rose scoffed out half a laugh and half a sob. "Right. And you're not frumpy. You've lost like, forty pounds, and have a handsome bull rider boyfriend—oh, sorry. Fiancé." Rose shook her head, realizing that she really was not fit company today. "I'm just going to go."

She turned, but Lily darted in front of her, which was saying something with how she carried Charlie. "You're not going."

"I've only lost twenty-nine pounds," Vi said. "And for a few months there, when Todd was taking his sweet time to ask me to marry him, I gained fifteen of that back."

"I finally did a German chocolate frosting intervention," Lily said.

Rose managed to chuckle a little, but she still didn't feel like hanging out with her sisters that day.

"The point is," Lily said. "We've all been where you are, and it's terrible. We understand. And you can't be alone right now. You need to be with us." Her voice broke on the last word, and Rose lifted her gaze to her oldest sister's.

"You need us, and we need you." Lily wiped her eyes quickly. "Right, Vi?"

"Right." Vi stepped to Lily's side, and they made a triangular huddle. "We love you, Rose. Things will work out with Liam."

Rose really didn't think they would, but she just nodded and said, "I've got to wash my face." Her eyes felt itchy and hot, and she really needed to blow her nose. Footsteps started down the steps, and she practically darted away from Lily and Vi so their mother wouldn't see her bawling her eyes out.

"Morning, girls," her mother's voice said behind her. "Is Rose here yet?"

"In the bathroom," Vi said a little too loudly. "She's not feeling well. Something about some bad Chinese."

Rose smiled as she ducked around the corner and went into the bathroom that sat between two of the bedrooms down there.

"Help me," she said to her reflection, the only prayer she could offer at the moment.

A couple of hours later, she stood on the top of the world, and it was glorious. She could see for miles in every direction, and the view was stunning, breath-taking, and spectacular.

The Grand Teton mountains towered above the valleys below, and the ride up on the gondola had shown them a few deer, as well as some beautiful countryside that couldn't be seen any other way.

She faced east, the wind whipping into her face, and imagined she could see Coral Canyon from the top of this mountain. She wondered if God felt like this, looking down on the people of Earth, wishing He could reach them all. Help them. Let them know He loved them.

In that moment, Rose felt the peace and love of God, and she took a long breath to hold onto the feeling.

"What do you think?" Vi asked, and Rose looked at her.

"I think it'll be freezing by December twenty-ninth. Covered in snow. And kind of ridiculous to make us all come up here for a five-minute ceremony." Beside her, Vi had her hood over her head, the strings drawn tight, and both hands in her jacket pockets.

"Because that's all you'll get," Rose said. "You'll be so cold."

"Yeah," Vi said. "It is beautiful, though."

"It is." Rose looked out across the world again. "But Vi, you just need somewhere we can all gather. There's not many of us, and Todd only has a few family members. You could have the wedding at the lodge."

"No." Vi shook her head. "Lily got married at the lodge."

"So? It doesn't have to be bigger and better."

"Is that so?" Vi shot her a venomous look that softened quickly. "And what would your wedding be like, Rose?"

She heard the hint of sarcasm in her name, and she took a few minutes to think about what she wanted in a wedding. "I'd find a nice reception center," she said. "Especially if I'd chosen a winter wedding date. I'd serve simple food that people would like. Salmon and rice pilaf, as well as short ribs and mashed potatoes." A smile touched her lips.

"There wouldn't be huge centerpieces, but just photos of me and—" She cut herself off before she could say Liam's name. "My husband," she said instead, her voice somewhat choked now. "And we'd have the ceremony, and eat dinner, and then I'd dance with Dad, and it would be done."

Vi looped her hand through Rose's elbow. "Sounds nice, Rose."

Rose leaned into her sister and watched the clouds fly through the sky, imagining walking toward Liam in his best, black tux, kissing him when she arrived at the altar, and then kissing him for the first time as his wife.

She wanted that fantasy to become reality so badly. So, so badly. But she couldn't make him choose her. He had to come to that decision on his own, and Rose couldn't even bring herself to pray for such a thing.

Liam was Liam, and she couldn't change him.

She felt like a completely different woman than the one who'd met him on that airplane all those months ago. A better person. One who finally knew who she was and what she wanted. So maybe there was still hope for Liam, but Rose wasn't going to wait around for him anymore.

"Rose, we're leaving," Lily called. "The gondola is going in ten minutes."

She took one long, last look at the view, and then she turned to go, hoping she could hold on to the peace she'd felt here, even for an extra moment.

And when she got back to the bottom of the mountain, and back to her house in Coral Canyon, she'd start looking for a man who wanted a family as much as she did.

CHAPTER 20

Liam rolled over when his alarm went off, slapping the nightstand to find his phone. He couldn't feel it, and his pounding headache and tight sinuses protested when he tried to sit up. He collapsed back to his pillows and let the alarm ring.

It didn't matter. He couldn't go into the clinic today anyway. Not with the infection raging through his system and making everything from breathing to eating painful. He'd been on an antibiotic for a couple of days now, but he honestly didn't feel that much better.

Maybe the kind of sickness he had couldn't be cured by modern medicine.

And the worst part? He didn't have a single person to call for help, and that only added to his misery. He finally got his fingers around his phone and cracked his eyelids enough to get the alarm off. The screen was so bright, and Liam just wanted to go back to sleep.

But he managed to send a text to both Arthur and Susan, read their responses that they'd call in Theo, and then he tossed his phone somewhere on the other side of the bed and rolled back over.

He couldn't breathe, and he ended up getting out of bed to

build up a fortress of pillows he could sort of sit and lean into, hoping to sleep without lying all the way flat.

What he really wanted was to call Rose and ask her to bring some chicken soup. Sit by him while he slept. Kiss him when he woke up.

He couldn't believe he hadn't seen her in a week, although he had to admit the anger over what she'd said had sustained him through the first seventy-two hours. After that, the sinus infection and double ear infections had taken over, and he hadn't been out of bed much since.

Plenty of time to obsess over what she'd said, really give it some good thought.

As your friend, I'm telling you that you need to quit at the clinic.

Every time he thought it, he rebelled at the idea of quitting. Maybe he didn't need to work so much. A day or two a week. He had three full-time doctors besides himself, and while the clinic was open sixteen hours a day, the three of them could cover it if he picked up a few shifts. Or hired someone else.

Now that the clinic had been deemed a big success, Liam had no doubt he could get more people to come to Coral Canyon. Maybe no one he'd worked with overseas, as they'd all ignored or avoided his phone calls.

Some of the most hurtful ones had been his colleagues he'd once shared every aspect of his life with. He pushed them away, the way he'd been doing for months now. He couldn't go back and change the past. He couldn't make Geoffrey tell the truth. Couldn't make the committee reverse their decision to let him go.

And honestly, he'd come out on top. Landed on his feet. Had somewhere to crash when everything had gone downhill. Not many other people could probably do that.

But other people probably had a family to find rest with. Liam's anger returned. He couldn't change who his family was, or why he'd felt like he couldn't tell them about his experiences in Nigeria.

He drifted in and out of consciousness, finally getting up

close to noon and dragging himself into the shower. The hot water helped to clear his sinuses, and when he went into the kitchen, he realized someone had been there.

A pot of soup sat on the counter with a note, and he glanced around before picking it up to read it. *Hope you feel better soon. Kami and Arthur.*

"See?" he said aloud to his big, empty house—and not even his house, but his parent's. "I have friends."

He heated up a bowl of soup and ate it alone in his kitchen. The silence allowed his mind to wander, and he let it go down forbidden paths—namely toward Rose.

In these quiet moments, some of what she'd said made sense. He'd been relying on his identity of a doctor for so long, that he didn't know how to be anything else.

He didn't know how to be Liam Murphy.

Because no one liked Liam Murphy. Liam Murphy didn't help people. He didn't know how to react to dangerous situations. He didn't know how to sleep beneath mosquito nets and decide who would get the last of the available medicine.

Doctor Murphy knew those things. Doctor Murphy commanded respect. Doctor Murphy had all the answers, to every question.

He couldn't stay in the summer cabin now that he was awake and up, so he left his soup bowl on the counter and got in his SUV. The LandRover sort of navigated itself down into town and toward the church where he'd been going each week.

After pulling into the parking lot, he sat in the truck with the engine running. The weather had started to turn toward winter, and he wasn't ready for that again. It seemed like summer had passed in the blink of an eye. There, then gone. He hadn't had time to go out on the lake as much as he would've liked. He hadn't taken Rose on any of the hikes he'd wanted to.

"Too busy at the clinic," he whispered to the windshield, regretting some of his decisions over the past few months.

But that didn't mean he had to *quit* completely. He could cut back.

Even as he thought it, Liam knew that wasn't true. He didn't do something halfway or part-time. If he did something, it consumed him, which was why he'd never had a successful relationship while also being a doctor.

Did he really have to choose his career or Rose?

Maybe another man wouldn't have to, but Liam felt way down deep in his gut that he would.

He sighed and flipped on his windshield wipers as it began to rain. His phone buzzed, and it wasn't Rose, so he almost didn't look at it. But he couldn't help himself. It could be someone from the clinic who needed him.

By some strange twist of fate or intervention from the Lord, it was his mother, asking how he was doing and that she hadn't heard from him in a while.

He'd get texts like this from her from time to time while he worked overseas too, and he wasn't sure if the line about not hearing from him was supposed to make him feel guilty, or if it was just an explanation for why she'd messaged.

His head hurt despite the medicine he'd taken, and he decided to be honest with her. *I'm really sick,* he sent back.

Oh, no, she responded. *What do you need?*

What did he need? He wasn't even sure himself, but he put the SUV in gear and started driving. An hour later, he pulled into his childhood driveway and faced the house he'd dreaded returning to.

He hadn't answered his mother, and she probably thought he'd either fallen asleep or was busy at work. Because Liam always worked, didn't he? Rain, shine, snow, mosquitoes, or floods, and Liam was at work.

And he was so, so tired. He just wanted to start enjoying his life, and for the first time since Rose had told him he needed to quit, he allowed himself to think she might be right.

He got out of his car and went up the imposing steps to the front door. He didn't knock or ring the bell but went straight in.

The scent of bacon and curry met his nose, and he knew immediately that his mother had started her chicken curry soup, probably for him. His heart started pounding in his chest as everything swirled inside him.

Sure enough, he found her in the kitchen, stirring a pot on the stove. "Hey, Mom," he said, his voice barely human. He'd never felt worse in his life, even after he'd learned that the committee in Geneva had decided to dismiss him.

"Liam." She left the spoon in the pot and came over to him. "You look awful, dear." She gathered him into a hug and held on tight. He hugged her back, using that force to keep himself from breaking down.

"Come on, now," she said after several moments. "Come sit down. The soup is almost ready. I was going to bring it to you."

Kami and Arthur had brought him soup too, but somehow his mother's was better. Different. Meant more.

As she walked back over to the stove, he noticed that she wore a pair of red-and-navy striped leggings with an overly large T-shirt. He'd never seen his mother wear anything like that. Anything that wasn't pressed and polished and perfectly tailored.

He stared for a moment, the sight before him so out of character, he didn't know what to make of it.

"Why did you come?" she asked. "You never answered my text."

"I don't know," he said, cradling his head in his hands and closing his eyes. If he could just get this pressure out of his head, everything would be fine. "Mom, I have to tell you something about my job with Doctors Without Borders."

She once again left the soup and came over to where he sat at the bar. "What is it?"

"I didn't leave," he said. "I was fired. Something happened in Nigeria, and I got blamed."

His mom didn't demand to know more, or ask if he'd really been at fault. She simply put her hands over his, and said, "I'm sorry."

"And I thought if I came here and opened that clinic, that I could prove that I was a good doctor."

"Oh, Liam, of course you're a good doctor."

He shook his head. "But I'm not. Good doctors know how to help people, and I don't even know how to be a person." As he spoke, he realized how right Rose had been. He had no idea who he was. A profession shouldn't define him, simply because he was good at it and enjoyed it.

Surely he'd be good at other things and enjoy them too.

"Tell me what you mean," his mother said, a line from his childhood he'd always hated but that he now appreciated.

"I mean, I know how to look at a chart or a patient and diagnose what's wrong with them. I know which drug will fix the problem. But I don't know…people. I don't know how to relax the way other people do, and I don't know how to be happy the way other people do. I thought if I just worked hard enough, the happiness would come." He sighed and looked at his mother. "But it hasn't." Something inside him snapped, and his chin trembled when he said, "I lost Rose, Mom."

"Oh, honey." She stood and gathered him into her arms again. Liam liked the comfort and strength within that circle, and he realized that he did have a very good mother. She'd done her best, the way most people did.

"Tell me what to do," he said.

His mom left him at the bar and went back to the soup. She pulled down a bowl from the cupboard and started ladeling. "First, you're going to eat this. Then you're going to tell me what happened with Rose, and we're going to figure out how you can get her back."

"Mom," he said. "I meant with…." What had he meant?

"Liam," she said, a bite in her voice. "I know you're a good doctor, whether you believe that or not. Rose knows it too. What she doesn't know is if you know how to be anything but a doctor."

She set the soup in front of him and opened a drawer to get a spoon. "You don't know how to be anything but a doctor either. And honey, she's not sick, and she doesn't need a doctor." She pushed his hair off his forehead, her touch cool to his fever. "She needs you."

Liam knew his mother was right. Now he just needed to figure out how to be Liam Murphy and not Doctor Murphy. It sounded easy in his head, but he knew it wouldn't be as simple as trading out a title.

CHAPTER 21

As the weeks passed and the trees lost their leaves, Rose grew accustomed to her new routine. She couldn't spend all day writing songs and wishing for a past that wasn't going to come back. Her sisters were happy in their new roles, and Rose wanted that for herself.

She didn't accept any invitations to dinner, because they mostly came from single dads dropping their kids off at the daycare where she'd taken a job. She wasn't opposed to marrying a man who already had a child, but she simply knew she wasn't ready to jump into another relationship so soon on the heels of the one ending with Liam.

She also knew, and only admitted to herself late at night when she couldn't sleep, that she was waiting for Liam to come back to her. Waiting, and hoping, and praying.

Because she worked in town now, she became acquainted with more people in Coral Canyon, and she'd heard through the gossip grapevine that Liam had quit at the clinic. Why he hadn't called her to tell her, she wasn't sure.

In her most desperate moments, she told herself it was because he hadn't fallen in love with her the way she had with him, and that he'd probably moved out of the summer cabin and was off on some grand life adventure.

She'd allowed herself to drive up Prospect Lake Road once, and she'd found his SUV in the driveway, so those insane thoughts had quieted.

Snow fell, and she answered Lily's call for help at the lodge. She and Beau wanted to make everything just right for Charlie's first Thanksgiving and Christmas, and Rose could definitely help make that happen.

She'd taken a pie-making class offered through the church, and she'd volunteered to make all the pies for Thanksgiving. Celia was on-hand to help, as Rose's last attempt at a pie had not gone super well.

"I think I've really improved," she said as she separated an egg.

"You have." Celia gave her a warm smile. "I'm not here to hover, Rose. If you need something, let me know." She lazily flipped a page in the recipe book she had on the counter in front of her.

"So just to make sure," Rose said. "One pumpkin, one pecan, and one chocolate mousse is going to be enough? How many people are coming?"

"Everyone except Eli," she said. "So that's six adults. Amanda and Jason." Celia started lifting fingers as she counted. "Todd and Vi. You, your parents."

That was up to thirteen adults.

"And the kids."

"Three littles, and Bayley," Rose said. "And you, right?"

"And me."

"But not Bree or Annie."

"I don't think they're coming this year, no," she said. "But there's—" She cut off and her eyes rounded. She quickly looked down at her book again. "Yeah, that's it."

"So three pies for fourteen people, plus kids. Should I maybe make another one?"

"What about this lemon chiffon?" She turned her book for Rose to see. "I could make that one."

Rose had never seen such a beautiful pie. "Yeah, you make that. I'll stick to the ones I can mix and dump into a shell." She gave a light laugh and added, "Okay, let's get this custard right this time."

It was the morning before Thanksgiving, so if the chocolate pie didn't turn out right this time, she had time to make it again. But things went well, and there were no lumps in the custard when she finished.

She took a finger full of the hot custard and put it in her mouth. "I think it's great," she said, offering the rubber spatula to Celia. She tasted it and said, "Yep. That's going to be perfect."

So Rose poured the filling into the cookie crust, and carefully pressed plastic wrap over it so it wouldn't get a skin.

Celia joined her in the kitchen after that, and they made a double batch of pie dough together. The hours passed, and they were enjoyable, with easy conversation and the scent of sugar and lemons and pumpkin.

During times like this, Rose didn't miss the music so much. She never wanted to go on tour again. And she knew that family and friends were more important than the next song, the money, or the fame she'd achieved in her life.

But back at her house, with everything quiet and dark and smelling like air freshener, she wondered again. Thankfully, she got up early and went right back to the lodge, where this time, the scent of roasting turkey filled the air.

"I'm here," she said to Celia when she walked in. She set her purse on the counter out of the way and grabbed her apron from the hook. Lily was already there too, her almost white hair pulled back out of her face.

"Hey, Rose." She beamed at her. "You ready for today?"

Rose took a deep breath and looked at all the moving parts in the kitchen. "I think so. I'm doing mashed potatoes and creamed corn, right?"

Celia had her hands wrist-deep in dough, and Rose couldn't even fathom doing that.

"Yes." Lily exchanged a look with Celia that Rose didn't understand. "And all the whipped cream for the pies."

"Oh, right." Rose turned away from the other two women. She positioned herself at the sink and started peeling what looked like fifty pounds of potatoes. After only doing two, she decided peeling wasn't her favorite chore. In fact, it made the muscles in her forearm ache, and she gripped the peeler extra hard so she wouldn't drop it.

Little by little, the meal came together, and Rose even managed to get her two side dishes hot and ready at the same time as everything else. Celia whisked the gravy one final time and said, "We're ready. Lily, go ring the bell."

"Ring the bell?" Rose asked, wiping her hair off her forehead. She'd probably just smeared something across her face, as she felt a bit sweaty and a little buttery. She'd stepped over to the sink to wash up when the loud, clanging sound of a cowboy dinner bell filled the air.

"Oh, wow," she said, but she couldn't even hear herself.

The bell stopped, but she just stood there, the ringing of it still echoing in her ears. People began pouring into the dining room, seemingly unfazed by the obnoxious noise they'd just endured.

The Whittakers had not rung this bell at any of the Christmas celebrations Rose had attended, and she realized that Thanksgiving dinner was obviously different. There were no name cards on the table, which Lily had set, and everyone stood behind their chair instead of sitting in it.

Lily came into the kitchen and said, "Look who I found," in a falsely bright voice. She stepped to the side to reveal Liam.

Rose gasped, her hand flying to her mouth. She started to shake, and she didn't even know why. Her stomach tightened, and every cell in her body stood at attention, ready for something to happen. Now, whether that was something exciting or something that would cause them pain, they weren't sure. But they were ready.

Liam looked *wonderful*, absolutely wonderful. Still as handsome as ever, with that clean-shaven face and those magnetic, ocean-colored eyes. He wore a simple pair of jeans with a button down shirt, a leather jacket over that, and that cowboy hat that took Rose's breath away.

"Hello, Rose," he said, that voice reaching right into her chest as if it were a hand and squeezing her heart. "Hello, everyone. Thanks for inviting me."

Inviting me?

Rose's gaze flew to Lily's and then Vi's. They both stood there smiling like this was a great moment. Rose wanted to slap them both and run out.

Becca stepped forward and said, "I invited him, Rose."

"What?" she asked, her brain trying to take in so much at once, and none of it made sense. She'd become great friends with Becca and Andrew over the months, as she'd babysat for them several times. Even Chrissy reached for her and said, "Rose."

Becca shifted the girl to her other hip and passed her to Andrew, who whispered something to her. "I've been working at the clinic as their new public relations director, and I found out he didn't have anywhere to go. So I invited him." She lifted her chin. "Everyone should have somewhere to go for Thanksgiving."

"He has parents," Rose said, her tone slightly acidic. Okay, maybe a lot more than slightly. She looked at Liam again, which was a huge mistake. He looked so...different, and yet exactly as she remembered him.

"I don't work at the clinic anymore," he said.

"I heard." She lifted her chin as if to tell him he wasn't the only one who'd made something of himself in Coral Canyon. "But not from you."

"I wanted to tell you," he said, taking a step toward her. "But I wanted to be the man you deserve before I talked to you again." He cut a glance at the audience they had, and when he looked at her again, she found vulnerability in his expression.

"I'm in love with you," he said. "And I'm not Doctor Murphy anymore."

Rose had no idea how he'd crossed the kitchen quite so quickly. But suddenly, he stood before her, one hand reaching up to push that errant hair off her forehead that she'd already moved with her greasy hands.

He ran both hands down her arms and laced his fingers between hers. Excitement poured through her, along with a heavy dose of anticipation.

"Who are you?" she whispered.

"I'm Liam," he said. "And I love you. I'm so, so sorry, Rose. Can we please try again?"

She knew he wasn't perfect, but he had just delivered the most perfect words, and the freeing feeling of forgiveness ran through her.

"Oh, come on," Lily said. "Kiss him."

Liam looked at her and then back to Rose. "What do you think?"

Rose squeezed his hands, a smile touching her mouth. "I think we can probably try again."

He leaned his forehead against hers, a simple, sensual movement. "I meant about the kissing."

Rose half-laughed, half-sobbed, and she tipped up on her toes at the same time Liam leaned down. This kiss ignited her blood and cemented the fact that while Liam might not be perfect, he was the perfect man for her.

Somewhere beyond them, cheers and laughter rang out, and Liam pulled away much sooner than she would've liked. He chuckled too, somehow having wrapped his arms around her during the kiss.

"Thanks for being my friend," he whispered.

"I love you," she whispered back, and then they faced their friends and family, who stood behind their chairs, clapping.

Embarrassment ran through her, especially when a tear escaped. She swiped at it quickly and waved for everyone to stop. "All right, all right," she said. "It's time to eat. Beau? Where's Beau?"

He stood down at the end of the table and lifted his hand. "Right here."

"You're in charge here. Let's say grace and get eating before everything gets cold."

"Yes, ma'am," he said, calling on Graham to say the prayer.

Rose ducked her head and leaned into the warmth of Liam, saying her prayer of gratitude to the Lord for bringing him back to her.

CHAPTER 22

Liam had never tasted such good food. His nerves buzzed at being so close to Rose, at being with so many friends as everyone passed the platter of turkey, the bowl of mashed potatoes, the creamed corn, the yams, the olives, the cranberry sauce, the rolls with jam, honey, butter. He'd never seen so much food.

"I made the mashed potatoes," Rose said among the other conversations. "And the corn, and the pies."

He forked up a piece of turkey and scooped some potatoes with it. "I'm sure they'll be delicious." He put the food in his mouth, honestly not sure what to expect. But it was salty and savory and creamy, and absolutely delicious. "Wow, this is great."

"Celia has trained me a little," she said. "And I took a pie class at church."

"I heard about that." Liam had a lot to tell her, but he didn't want to get into his therapy with so many other people so closeby.

Dinner passed quickly, at least to Liam, and he engaged in several conversations with those around him, namely Becca and Andrew, who had been more than welcoming. When Becca had invited him, he'd flat out refused. He knew Rose wouldn't want him there, and he didn't want to try to make up with her in front of everyone.

But Becca could be very convincing, and before he knew it, he'd said yes. He'd planned to contact Rose before Thanksgiving, but he'd never been able to figure out how. Would she answer if he called? Should he stop by the daycare, where he knew she'd taken a job?

In the end, he'd done nothing and Thanksgiving had come. He'd tried texting Becca that morning, but she'd beat him to it. He'd woken up to two texts from her and they'd said the same thing, the second time in all-caps.

Don't even think about canceling today. I'll see you at noon.

So Liam had showered and taken care of his responsibilities and shown up at the lodge at noon. After all, he knew Becca would drive down to his place and get him if he didn't.

"I'll put the coffee on," Celia said, and Liam realized that a few people had gotten up to take their dishes into the kitchen. He stayed at the table and leaned toward Rose.

"Thanks for not throwing me out." Though she'd said she loved him, Liam wasn't sure that wasn't just because she'd been put on the spot.

She slipped her hand into his under the table and said, "You seem different."

"I feel different." He glanced at Lily as she reached for his plate. "I can get it." He stood and took his plate and then grabbed Rose's too. He took the dishes into the sink, dodging a few people.

Lily grabbed onto his arm before he could turn back to the table. "I'm so glad you came," she said quietly. "She was so surprised." She sounded giddy.

"I don't think that was a good thing," Liam said, smiling at her.

"Oh, it was," Lily said. "Rose loves surprises."

Liam hoped that was true, because he had a lot of them yet to reveal. Lily started getting out mugs and putting them on the counter. Beau pulled an assortment of creamers out of the fridge, and Celia put the sugar bowl on the counter too.

He caught Rose's eye just before she slipped out of the dining room. He left through the other kitchen exit, and they met in the hall.

"You want to go downstairs for a bit?" she asked.

"Sure." He followed her away from the fray in the kitchen, his nerves returning. Once they were alone, she turned and kissed him again. Her fingers explored the sides of his face, as if she was trying to make sure he was the same man she'd dated before.

"I have a lot to tell you," he said when she pulled away.

"All right. Let's sit." She didn't go into the theater room, where all the recliners were, but chose to stay out in the living area and sat on the couch.

He joined her and clasped his hands together. "So I've been seeing a counselor for a few months now."

The shock appeared on Rose's face, and she blinked rapidly. "You have?"

"Yeah." He started nodding. "Yep. I had a lot to work out from my last job. And the clinic. And my family." He exhaled. "It's been a pretty rough couple of months." Especially without her. But he didn't want to tell her that. Rose shouldn't be made to think that she could've solved his problems. That wasn't fair to her, and his counselor had told him specifically not to put that weight on her.

"Who are you seeing?"

"A work crisis counselor," he said. "She's here in town. Her name's Toni Thompson."

"And you like her?"

"I do." He looked at Rose. "And I got a dog."

"You did not." She grinned and burst into laughter. "That's so great, Liam."

He smiled too. "She's great too. She's a former therapy dog, and her name's Daffodil. Felt like we were a perfect match." He wasn't sure if she'd get the significance of the name, but the way her eyes shone, he thought she did.

"Daffodil," she said. "That does seem perfect."

"And I moved."

"Out of the summer cabin?"

"That's right." He popped the T and tucked her hair behind her ear. "You want to come see?"

"Of course I do." She stood like they'd leave right then.

Liam chuckled and looked up at her. "Right now?"

"Yes, right now." She tugged on his hand until he stood. "We can have pie and coffee when we get back. Why didn't you bring your dog with you?"

"I wasn't sure if I could."

"Of course you can. There are dogs wandering all over the place here." She started for the steps, and Liam went with her. She told Celia where they were going, and they went outside.

Liam drove slowly down the canyon, and not because the roads were terribly bad. They weren't, as it hadn't snowed a ton in Coral Canyon yet. But because his stomach felt like he'd eaten way too much turkey.

He wasn't sure why he was worried about Rose liking his new house or not. Dr. Thompson would've told him that was something outside of his control, and he shouldn't focus on it. So he pushed away the anxiety and drove right past Prospect Lake Road.

"I came up here once," she said. "Just to make sure you hadn't left town."

"Oh yeah? Why would you think I'd left town?"

"I'd heard you quit at the clinic, and I couldn't believe you'd stay here if you weren't doing that."

Her gaze on the side of his face felt like a ton of bricks. He looked at her, finding her blue eyes so open and honest. So questioning.

"It was very hard to leave the clinic," he finally said, turning at the stop sign at the bottom of the canyon. "And it took me some time to realize that you were right. I might have a medical degree, but being a doctor does not define who I am."

"I didn't mean to make you feel bad."

"Sometimes the truth hurts." He gave her a smile so she'd know whatever had happened between them was fine. In the past. Over. "Anyway, I bought a place closer to town. I got a dog. I work in the garden, and take Daffodil into the mountains, and I do some online medical consulting with a couple of research organizations, just to fill my time."

"Wow," she said. "I had no idea you knew how to garden."

"Well, I took a class at the nursery." He tossed her another smile. "Apparently, you're not the only one who can sign up for a class."

She laughed, and he pulled into a modest, brown-brick rambler and cut the engine. "This is it."

"This is it?" She got out of his SUV, but Liam took a moment to take a deep breath of the interior of the car. Yep, it smelled like her floral perfume, and a blast of happiness hit him hard.

He joined her as she walked slowly up the front sidewalk. "I put in a lot of bulbs this fall, so next spring, these flowerbeds should be spectacular."

"I can't wait to see that."

He led her up the steps and through the front door. It was a typical rambler, with a small foyer, an expansive living room which connected to the dining room and kitchen. Daffodil came clicking over, her claws on the hard floor always announcing her presence.

"This is Daffodil." He scratched the dog behind the ears and got a goofy smile from the animal in return. He loved her, and she loved him, kept him company, and listened to him talk things through without judgment.

"Oh, she's beautiful." Rose knelt in front of the black lab and started rubbing her down. "Have you been taking good care of Liam? Have you?"

Daffodil gave him a look like, *Why don't you ever pet me like this?* and leaned into Rose like they were old pals.

Liam just laughed and took Rose down the hall toward the three bedrooms down there. "This is my room. It has a bathroom. This is a guest bedroom. This, I think would be nice for a nursery. Bathroom here." He went back the way he came, saying, "There's a basement too. It's not as nice as the lodge's, but I love spending time down there."

He paused, realizing Rose had not come with him. He retraced his steps and found her still standing outside the bedrooms. The doors all sat across from one another, like a crossroads or a game of *Which room shall I choose?*

"Rose?" he asked.

She looked at him, her eyes wide and her chin trembling. "Nursery?"

"Yeah." He approached and drew her into his side, facing the smallest of the three bedrooms up here. "Now that I'm not a crazy person, working a million hours a week, I think I could be a decent dad."

"You don't want kids."

"Well, Doctor Murphy didn't want kids." He looked at her again. "But *I* would very much like to have a lot of little girls that look just like you."

Her tears fell then, and Liam pulled her into a tight hug. She cried for only a few moments, and then she collected herself and said, "All right. Let's go see the basement."

Liam had never felt so lucky. He'd never been more grateful for the gift of forgiveness. He could only hope that he'd continue to be able to make Rose understand that he was the kind of man she wanted and needed, and that he could be that man for her.

———

The following day, every retail establishment on the planet was having a sale. Liam had decided to take full advantage and go into the only jewelry store in Coral Canyon. Rose liked surprises, and he wanted to have a diamond in his pocket every day until he felt like the time was right to ask her to be his wife.

He was fairly confident she'd say yes, but he wanted the moment to be perfect. And to do that, he needed the perfect ring. He'd seen her wear more gold than silver, and she wasn't afraid of big pieces, long, dangly earrings, or lots of jewels.

After explaining all of this—and the fact that it could not be common knowledge that he'd bought a ring—the saleswoman took him over to a case of engagement rings that she thought might be appropriate.

"These are nice," Sandi said, pulling out a long, thin tray of rings. "They're larger, with thicker bands, and some of the cuts and arrangements are one-of-a-kind."

Like Rose was. Liam had a panicked thought that she should be here with him to ensure she got exactly what she wanted. But he also had a desire to choose something he thought she'd like. So he looked, and he asked questions, and in the end, he purchased a ring that looked a lot like a flower, with dozens of smaller gems inlaid around the main diamond.

Now all he had to do was find the perfect moment to surprise her.

CHAPTER 23

R ose became the one with no time over the next few weeks. If she wasn't working at the daycare, she was up at the lodge helping with Vi's wedding plans. She'd opted to get married at the reception center in town, and the sisters were making all the centerpieces, bouquets, and other flower arrangements themselves.

All the nieces and nephews needed matching clothes, and Rose sat with her mother while she sewed dresses for the girls and ties for the boys. She listened to Vi talk about moving into Todd's house, selling another home, and starting her new life.

And Rose was happy for her. She saw Liam in the evenings, when he brought Daffodil to her house with a box of pizza or a couple of bags of Chinese takeout.

"We're decorating the lodge and tree tomorrow," she told him about a week before Christmas. "If you want to come. The Christmas traditions are kind of a big deal up at Whiskey Mountain Lodge."

"I've heard," he said, as Rose had told him about her last two Christmases there.

"So you should come," she said. "It's great to see everyone working together and getting along."

"All right," he said. So the next day, they drove up to the lodge together, where the Christmas spirit was already going strong. Holiday music played through the whole lodge, and the scent of chocolate and cider hung in the air.

Graham, Beau, and Andrew hung the highest ornaments on the tree while Todd hung the garland above the fireplace and down the railing, under Vi's watchful eye. Rose, Liam, and Lily hung the lower ornaments, and Celia called everyone into the kitchen for homemade doughnuts and hot drinks before the work was finished.

Rose basked in the familial love these people had for each other, for their strong traditions, and for their willingness to let anyone in to experience it all. Becca started a batch of gingerbread cookies with Bayley and the other kids, and Rose went back into the living room to put out the nativities with a couple of other people.

With everyone working together, it didn't take long for the lodge to come to life with holiday spirit.

She turned to find Liam in an engrossing conversation with Lily, Vi, and Becca, and her radar went off. Loudly.

"Hey," she said. "Are we going down to town for lunch?" That had been the plan, but it looked like this quad had just come up with a different idea.

Vi stepped in front of Liam, who wore a look halfway between anxiety and excitement on his face. "Rose, we have something we want to talk to you about."

"Yeah," Lily said, joining Vi and making a wall of protection for Liam.

"What's going on?" Rose asked, more wary than anything else.

"I bought you a ring," Liam said, muscling his way through the other two Everett sisters. He produced said ring with a flourish, and Rose sucked in a tight breath at the sight of it.

"It kind of looks like a rose," he said. "And I've been holding onto it for a few weeks now, watching for the perfect time to ask you to marry me."

"And I told him he should do it quick so you could get married with me," Vi said, hipping him sideways a couple of inches.

Rose looked back and forth between them. "What?" The word came out as mostly air, because what they were saying made no sense.

"We have the best venue," Lily said. "All the plans have been made. Everyone will already be there, well." She looked at Liam. "Besides Liam's parents, but he just got done saying they'd come if he called them."

Rose blinked and took a moment to get control of her emotions. "But Vi's getting married in ten days."

"And you should be too," Vi said. "You two love each other, and trust me when I say it's torture to have a long engagement."

Becca finally stepped into the conversation, and said, "Then you can get started on having all those babies you want."

Heat filled Rose's whole body. "I can't get married in ten days. It's absurd."

"Why not?" Liam asked. "You told me the other night you don't care what your wedding is like, as long as I show up. And I'll already be at Vi and Todd's wedding."

"Vi," Rose said with a note of pleading in her voice. "This is your big day. You don't want to share it with me."

"I told you," she said to Lily. "Rose, let's talk for a minute, okay?" She put her arm around Rose's shoulders and led her away from the group. In the dining room, they found Todd, who glanced up from his phone.

"Everything set for the double wedding?"

Rose's mouth dropped open. "You're in on this too?"

He chuckled and gave Vi a quick kiss on the cheek. "Honestly, Rose. We don't care about having the day to ourselves. We just want to get married, and Vi's convinced that's all you want too. She thinks you might elope with Liam at the courthouse, and she doesn't want that to happen."

Rose looked at Vi, really trying to understand. "You don't?"

"Of course not," Vi said. "I want to be at your wedding, celebrating with you." She took both of Rose's hands. "Come on, Rose. All you need is a dress, and we can get one of those today."

"Today?" Everything was happening so fast. Too fast.

"Didn't Liam show her the ring?" Todd asked, pure confusion in his voice.

"I think we hit her with too many surprises at once," Vi responded. "Let's give her a minute." She trailed her fingers along Rose's arm and said, "We'll send in Liam."

Then she and Todd left, and Rose stood in the dining room, wondering if she was living in her reality, if she was asleep, or if she'd somehow entered an alternate dimension.

Then Liam was there, and he got down on one knee and held out the ring. "I love you, Rose. Will you *please* marry me in ten days?"

Gazing down at that huge diamond, and those gorgeous eyes, Rose found she couldn't think of a single reason why she couldn't. So she said, "Yes," a slightly maniacal laugh following the word.

Liam grinned, chuckled, and stood to put the engagement ring on her finger. "This is going to be great. You'll see."

———

AFTER THE ANNUAL CHRISTMAS TREE LIGHTING CEREMONY, WHICH Charlie and Chrissy led, and the delicious Christmas Eve dinner, and the stocking gift exchange, Rose gave herself a day off. Then she was right back to finding the perfect pair of shoes and discussing how she should wear her hair for her wedding.

Her wedding.

A year ago, she'd been nothing but jealous of her sisters,

lamenting the fact that she still lived in Nashville, and wondering when she'd ever find the just-right man for her.

She couldn't believe how much things had changed in only a year, nor how much *she'd* changed. She hardly recognized her life, or herself.

She was so much better than she'd ever been, and happier, and she couldn't wait to marry the man of her dreams.

Then one morning, she woke up, and it was time to do exactly that. She let her mother help her into her dress, which was simple in the fact that it was form-fitting, without lace or fancy buttons. A zipper up the back, a veil over her curled and pinned-up hair, and a bouquet of red roses.

Roses for Rose. It was all she'd ever wanted, and as she stood in the bride's room with Vi, she almost started crying.

"Vi, you're so kind to let me do this with you," she said, her voice breaking on every other word.

"Rose, don't cry yet," she said. "Okay? You'll ruin your makeup, and then Beth will be so upset."

Beth was Vi's makeup artist, and Rose had just tagged along, paid her extra, and got her makeup done too.

She took a deep breath. "All right."

Her mother knocked and came in, and said, "Rose, come with me quickly."

Rose moved, knowing she only had a matter of a minutes to get out of this room and into a waiting room that had been set up for her to watch Vi get married. The event coordinator at the reception center would then come for Rose.

Her mom led her down a hall and opened a door, saying, "I'll see you in there, dear," before rushing off.

Rose went in the room, glad she didn't have long skirts or anything fancy that she needed help with. She'd taken two steps into the room, the door just closing behind her when she realized she wasn't alone.

Liam turned from where he stood in front of the monitor showing Todd standing at the altar, waiting for Vi.

"Oh, no," Rose groaned. "I'm not supposed to see you before the wedding."

"It's okay," he said, walking forward, his dark-as-midnight tux seeming like it had been made just for him. Of course, it probably had been. "We're watching in here together." He grinned and took her hand, standing back as he drank her in.

"I am the luckiest man in the world."

Rose almost started crying again. "Stop it."

"Let's go watch," he said as the wedding march started to play. She stood beside him, this man she adored, and watched as her sister said her vows and kissed her husband. She dabbed at her eyes, the happiest she'd ever been in her life.

"Our turn," Liam said softly, lifting her hand to his lips. He took her out of the room and down the hall. He peeked through the door, while Rose had expected someone else to do all of this. She realized that Liam had been busy planning behind her back —again.

"My whole life from now on is going to be a series of surprises, isn't it?" she asked him.

"I certainly hope so," he said with a mischievous grin. "I think they're ready for us. Are you ready?"

Was she ready to be Liam's wife?

"I was born ready," she said, linking her elbow through his.

He chuckled, pressed his lips to her forehead, and said, "I love you."

"And I love you."

Then he opened the doors, the wedding march played, and Liam walked her down the aisle to the altar.

———

Read on for a sneak peek at **HER COWBOY BILLIONAIRE BLIND DATE**, which features the Whittaker boys' mother, Amanda! **It's available for you to read in paperback.**

SNEAK PEEK! HER COWBOY BILLIONAIRE BLIND DATE CHAPTER ONE

Amanda Whittaker sighed as she closed the door, turning and letting her eyes flutter shut as she sagged into the wood behind her. She wondered what Ryder was doing on the other side. He'd certainly seemed stunned, and Amanda actually was too.

They'd been out four times now, and she just didn't feel a spark with him. At age sixty-two, she didn't have time to date a man she didn't feel much for, even if she enjoyed spending time with someone besides her poochon. And that wasn't even a someone. The little black poodle Bichon Frise mix certainly didn't speak English.

She did balance on Amanda's knee and whine, excited her master was home. Amanda bent down and said, "Hey, baby," scooping the little dog into her arms. She moved away from the door as she continued. "I broke up with Ryder tonight. Just now, actually."

Right when he'd leaned in to kiss her.

Another sigh leaked from her mouth.

Maybe I shouldn't have broken up with Jason.

It was not the first time the thought had crossed her mind in the past six months. She'd spent three Christmases with Jason. Two and a half years. He was a good man, and she'd loved him. She believed he loved her. But the man had a serious temper, and he'd lost his son because of some terrible things he'd said and done.

And he was completely unrepentant, and he'd stopped going to church years ago. They'd talked about faith and religion dozens of times, and in the end, he just couldn't come back. Didn't want the same things she did.

Seeing no other choice, she'd ended their relationship. Since then, she'd been lonelier than ever, second only to the months after her husband had died.

She allowed herself to weep as she fed Beans and refilled the little dog's water bowl. She'd curl up in bed and Beans would lay right against her hip, and Amanda would figure out what to do in the morning.

Sunday morning, which she'd spend at church and then she'd go to lunch at Whiskey Mountain Lodge with her sons, their wives, families, and friends.

She wouldn't be alone, and she was infinitely grateful for that.

The following morning, she slipped on her heels and said to Beans, "I'll be back later, Beany Baby," and headed out to her car. At least it was summer, and she didn't have to worry about driving in snow.

Despite living in Wyoming for her entire adult life, Amanda didn't particularly enjoy winter, and if the snow and wind was bad, she didn't leave the house. After all, she didn't have to. She had no job, no obligations besides those she chose. Visiting friends, or serving people in her church, or helping a neighbor down the street with yard work or baking or making cards for their grandchildren.

She and Ronald had worked hard to provide a good life for their boys, and when he'd died, Amanda and all the children had become billionaires. And yet, money couldn't seem to help find her a man that she wanted to spend the rest of her life with.

She set aside the thoughts as she went into the chapel. Beau and Lily always saved her a spot on the end of the row, and she hated how it was twice as much room as she needed. Of course, she'd been coming to church with Ryder for a week or two now, and she hadn't sent any texts about the break-up.

"I'll take Charlie," she whispered as she sat down, leaving several inches of space between her and her son.

"Hey, Ma," he said, looking behind her. "No Ryder today?"

"We broke up," she said, gesturing for him to hand her the baby. Charlie had just turned eighteen months, and his chubby cheeks and quick smile disguised the fact that he'd spent several weeks in the NICU as a preemie.

"Broke up?" Beau took Charlie from Lily and passed him to Amanda.

She grinned at the baby and kissed him. He was so perfect, and she loved her grandchildren with everything in her. Beau set the diaper bag on the bench between them. "I thought you liked him."

"I did," Amanda said, glancing up to the pulpit and hoping the pastor would start soon so she wouldn't have to answer her son's questions. It wouldn't matter if it was now or later. She'd have to answer them. "I do."

"Did he break up with you?"

"No," she said. "There was just no...connection there."

"Mom," Beau said, his eyes alight with concern.

"I'm fine," she said. "We went out four times."

"You should let me and Graham set you up," he said. "He knows tons of guys, and—"

"I don't want a *guy*," Amanda said, throwing a glare in Beau's direction. "And I don't want to be set up." It wasn't the first time Beau had suggested such a thing. Amanda hadn't had any problems getting her own dates, thank you very much. The problem was, she hadn't had any luck choosing the right men either.

Men, not guys.

She wasn't flirty and thirty, or even forty and fabulous. Heck, fifty was in her rear-view mirror.

The sermon started, and Beau focused his attention up front —or on Lily. She wasn't sure which, but Amanda didn't mind. She got to cuddle with her grandson and feed him crackers and listen to the pastor talk about treating everyone with respect.

About halfway through the sermon, her phone buzzed in her purse, and she pulled it out. Graham, her oldest son, had texted. *No Ryder today? Beau says you broke up.*

Amanda rolled her eyes, sure Graham would somehow be able to feel it. And she wasn't dignifying his text with a response. He didn't need one. Ryder's absence on the bench was confirmation enough.

"Stop texting your brother," she hissed to Beau, who simply smiled at her and then looked back up to the dais. She didn't hear much of the sermon after that, and she took Charlie with her out into the lobby.

His other grandma waited there, with his grandpa, and she passed the baby to Jack Everett with a smile. "Do you want to ride up to the lodge with us?" Fran asked, taking the diaper bag from Amanda.

"I think I'm going to go with Vi today," she said, looking around. "She wanted me to talk to her about making a coconut cream pie for Todd's birthday."

Sure enough, one of the blonde Everett sisters came out of the chapel with her arm through her husband's. She brushed her short hair back and asked, "Amanda, you're coming with us, right?"

"Yep." Vi and Todd lived in town, so they'd be coming back this way later, and Amanda rode up to the lodge with them often. Or another of the Everetts, as it made no sense for so many to drive up the canyon only to drive back down.

Beau and Lily appeared, and Amanda was suddenly anxious to leave. She didn't want to get bombarded with more break-up questions, and she inched toward the door. But Graham exited the chapel on the other side and made a beeline for her before she could get very far.

He carried little Ronnie in his arms, and he said, "Mom, I know just the guy for you."

"Man," Beau said, nudging Graham. "He knows just the *man* for you, Mom."

She looked back and forth between her sons, her patience so thin with them already. Perhaps she should just go home today. Heat up some leftovers. Snuggle with Beans and a pot of coffee.

Beau and Graham looked at her with bright eyes filled with hope, and Amanda wanted to give them the world, same as she always had.

She sighed, knowing she was about to regret the words that came out of her mouth.

"Fine," she said. "Set it up."

————

A WEEK LATER, AMANDA HAD TRIED EVERYTHING IN HER POWER TO get out of the blind date Graham had arranged for her. He wouldn't even tell her the name of the man he knew, and Amanda was beginning to think he didn't know anyone.

But hey, she hadn't heard the word guy again. It was always, *Mom, I promise you'll like this man,* or *Mom, this man is perfect for you.*

After her son's texts, maybe she was hopeful. She also knew how dangerous hope could be, and she tried not to hold onto it too tightly.

She knew there were apps for older singles like her, but she wasn't ready to go there yet. She really just wanted a calm man. One with good values and morals. One who could support himself. Who just needed someone to talk to at night, the way she did. One ready to love, even if it only lasted for a few years.

"That was Jason's problem," she murmured as she put her earrings on. "He wasn't ready to let go of the past and love."

She'd told Graham and Beau very early on *No cowboys. No one in their forties.*

That had sparked one of Graham's most disturbing messages from that week.

How young can I go?

Jason had been ten years younger than her, so she said fifty-two, and then begged Graham to tell her who he was thinking of setting her up with.

He'd done no such thing, and she was meeting this mystery man at Devil's Tower in thirty minutes, just as Beau had directed her. He'd also said *Mom, every man in Wyoming is a cowboy. How non-cowboy are we talking?*

She hadn't answered, because a few minutes later, Graham had given more details about the date. She was supposed to wear her silver scarf, which was ridiculous this close to June, but that was what her son had said.

Between the two of them badgering her, Amanda had decided to just roll with it. Wear what they said to wear. Be where they said to be.

She draped the silver scarf over her blue sweater, and the two colors really worked with her dark hair salted with gray and her dark blue eyes.

That squirrel of hope moved through her again, and she took a deep breath to contain the giddy feeling in her stomach she got whenever she went out with a new man. There was always such an excitement, even if she didn't know who he was.

Twenty-eight minutes later, she pulled into Devil's Tower and clicked across the parking lot to the front doors. She wasn't an idiot, and she'd seen Beau's truck in the back of the lot, almost like he'd been trying to hide it.

She didn't see him inside, nor Graham, and she gave her

name to the hostess. "Right this way, Mrs. Whittaker," the girl said, despite there being several couples obviously waiting for a table.

She was seated in a booth over on the side, away from the doors but with a good view of the park across the street from the restaurant. Nerves hit her then, and she wondered how long she'd have to wait.

"Something to drink?" a man asked, easily thirty or forty years younger than Amanda.

She gave him a kind smile and said, "Yes, please. I'll have a frozen raspberry lemonade."

The young man left, and she casually looked at the menu, noting that the hostess had put down a second one across from her, as if she knew Amanda would be meeting someone.

A few minutes later, the waiter put her lemonade down and said, "I'll be right back, ma'am," leaving her with the bright pink concoction.

She ripped the wrapper off the straw and swirled it through the drink before taking a sip. It was perfectly sour and sweet and delicious, and she sighed. Maybe this blind date wouldn't be so bad.

Please let this be the one, she prayed. She picked up her glass again, the chill of it against her fingers reminding her to take a deep breath. Everything would be okay. But she'd never had this much trouble finding someone she liked. She'd married her husband when she was only eighteen, and after only a few months of dating.

"Amanda?" a man asked.

She swung her head toward the man standing at the end of the table. He didn't look like a cowboy, thank goodness.

She didn't know him, but he was tall, with sandy hair and the brightest pair of blue eyes she'd ever seen. They sparkled at her, and she lost the words that had been in her mind.

"I'm Finley Barber," he said, extending his hand for her to shake. "I think you're my date for the night. Silver scarf." He grinned, and Amanda's pulse went nuts. He was handsome, and she wondered where in the world Graham and Beau had found him.

She stuck her hand out, realizing a moment too late that she was holding that raspberry lemonade.

Horror struck her as the thick, red liquid went flying, hitting the gorgeous man right in the abdomen.

SNEAK PEEK! HER COWBOY BILLIONAIRE BLIND DATE CHAPTER TWO

Things had been moving in slow motion for Finley Barber. His truck wouldn't seem to go over forty miles per hour the whole way from Dog Valley. His feet seemed to be going backward as he walked into Devil's Tower.

And getting to the table with the pretty woman wearing the silver scarf? It had taken a year.

As soon as that ice cold drink hit his skin, though, everything rushed forward. Before he knew it, Amanda had scooted out of the booth. "I'm so sorry," she said, grabbing her napkin and pressing it against his stomach.

Everyone in the vicinity was looking at them, and Finn tried to smile. But wow, that stuff was *cold*.

"It's fine," he said, taking the napkin and stepping back. "Really."

A waiter appeared, and he handed Finn his black towel. "I'll get you another drink, ma'am." Another man appeared, and he swept away the tipped glass and all the liquid in the blink of an eye.

"Would you like something to drink?" the waiter asked, and Finn blinked, trying to get all the pieces aligned in his head.

"I'll bring some water," the waiter said, and he left Finn and

Amanda alone. She let out a shaky laugh and wiped her palms down the front of her thighs.

"I'm so sorry," she said again. "I don't know what I was thinking."

He wiped the slush off his shirt and said, "It's just a polo. I own a washing machine." He gestured to the bench where she'd been sitting. "Please. Sit down."

She did, which allowed Finn to do the same. He left the towel at the end of the table and looked at Amanda. She had beautiful eyes, dark like the blue depths of the ocean. Her shoulder-length hair held swirls of gray, and he really liked that she didn't try to cover them up. Hide them underneath dyes and chemicals.

"So you're Graham's mother," he said, adding a smile to it. He could clearly see the shape of Graham's nose in Amanda, as well as feel it in the energy she put off.

"That's right," she said. "I'm Amanda Whittaker."

"He didn't tell me I'd be meeting his mother." Finn wasn't sure what he'd have done differently. *Maybe said no*, he thought. After all, he valued his friendship with Graham and Laney, and if his mother didn't like him, would that be broken?

"Yes, well, he didn't tell me anything either," Amanda said, glancing up when the waiter set down a fresh slushy drink.

"Have you had a chance to look at our drink menu?" he asked.

Finn had not, but he said, "Bring me one of those too, would you please?"

"Sure thing."

"It's frozen raspberry lemonade," Amanda said as the waiter walked away.

"Sounds great," Finn said. He leaned closer like he was about to share a very deep secret. "I haven't been on a date in a while. I'm pretty rusty."

"Oh, that's okay," Amanda said, sticking her straw in her slush. "I've been out loads of times." Her eyes widened. "I mean

—I—my husband died six years ago, and I've dated a few men since then."

Finn nodded. "I know about Graham's father."

"Do you have children?" she asked. The silver-haired dating scene had plenty of divorces, widows, and children—grandchildren even. Not that Finn would know. He spent the majority of his time with equines, dogs, and chickens.

Amanda did not seem like the kind of woman to appreciate any of those things, and he wished his heart wasn't beating so fast. She was mighty pretty though, and Finn hadn't been out with anyone in a couple of years. Not since Kristen had stuck around long enough for him to fall in love with her, only to find out she was really interested in his bank account and not being his wife.

"Finley?" she asked.

"Finn," he said. "I go by Finn. Two N's."

She smiled again and took a sip of her drink. "Okay, Finn. Do you have children?"

"Yes," he said, getting his brain to work. "I've got two daughters. Joann is thirty, and Kimberly is twenty-seven. They live in Jackson Hole. My ex-wife lives there too."

She nodded, absorbing the information without a trace of judgement on her face. Finn appreciated that. "And where do you live? I think I'd know if you were here in Coral Canyon."

"Would you?" he asked, grinning at her. "How's that?"

"Well, I've lived here for almost forty-five years. This place isn't that big."

"It's gotten a lot bigger recently," he said, glancing out the window as if the evidence of town growth would be right there.

"True," Amanda said. "But I still think I'd know if there was a handsome man like you in town. Available."

His gaze flew back to hers. *Handsome?* She really was better at this dating thing than he was. "I live in Dog Valley," he said. "I own a boarding stable out there." She didn't need to know that he came from one of the richest racehorse stables in the country.

Or that, years ago, he'd invented the software she probably used to do her online banking. Or that the horses he bred, trained, and worked with sold for hundreds of thousands of dollars.

No one needed to know that. At least not right now.

"Dog Valley," she said, that smile showing all her straight, white teeth. "That's great."

"Yeah?" he asked. "It's thirty minutes away from here."

"Less staring," she said with a definite hint of flirtation in her voice.

Finn laughed, wishing he'd worn his cowboy hat. Graham had warned him against it though, saying the woman he was meeting needed to be "eased in" to the idea of dating a cowboy.

Finn had almost called it off right then. He *was* a cowboy. He'd been born with spurs on. Dust for blood. The sound of horse's hooves clomping in his nursery at night.

"Oh, I think you'll find plenty of people staring in Dog Valley," he said. "Remember how I said I hadn't been out with anyone in a while?" He shook his head, glad when his frozen drink came too, and he had something else to focus on.

"People know you then?" she asked.

"Yes," he said simply. "People out there know me."

She kept the smile in place, and Finn let her ask another question, hoping he could live up the standards of this woman, get her number for himself, and set up a second date real soon.

———

"And she has grandkids," he told Vanilla, the yellow lab who followed him everywhere. Chocolate and Licorice had gotten sick of the date recap about ten minutes ago, but Finn was still floating on air.

He'd just gone on a date for the first time in two years, and it wasn't horrible. In fact, it was downright amazing, and he had left Devil's Tower with Amanda's number in his phone and the promise to call her dripping from his lips.

"She's a little older than me," he told Vanilla as he shut off all the lights and made sure the doors were locked. He had three Labrador retrievers, and they'd definitely alert him if there was a problem. Not that Finn expected any. His land was pretty remote, with the nearest neighbor living five miles away.

But sometimes wild animals ventured onto his property, scaring the horses. He made sure they were all locked properly in the barn each night, because losing one was like losing an entire year's salary.

"I just can't believe we hit it off," he said. "I honestly wasn't expecting to like her. I was only doing it as a favor to Graham." When his friend had called and said he had the perfect date for Finn, he'd almost said no.

But something in him had made him pause and listen. "He still should've said it was his mother, don't you think?"

Vanilla didn't answer, just clicked alongside Finn as he went down the hall to the master suite. Chocolate and Licorice were curled up on the right side of the bed, practically on top of one another. Vanilla jumped up there next to them, circled around, and flopped down.

"You guys will have to move so I can get the covers," he said, their nightly routine. Of course, the dogs would not move. They were three of the most stubborn canines on the planet, almost like they prided themselves on being wonderful, loyal, and downright maddening.

If Finn had a bit of liver pinched between his fingers, all three of them would do whatever he said. And they were great with the horses, and Licorice could even herd the chickens.

"Go on," he said. "Move." He had to heave the dogs off the bed one by one to get his blanket out from under them, and then he fell asleep almost instantly, a smile on his face for the first time in a long, long time.

The following morning, Finn forced himself to work through his morning chores as normal. Set a pot of coffee to brew as normal. Set bread in the toaster. Take his vitamins. Send a couple of texts to his daughters.

It was Sunday, so he showered and as he walked down the hall, adjusting his tie, he decided he'd waited long enough to call Amanda.

Weren't men supposed to call the next day?

He wasn't sure what time she'd be at church, though they had talked about her pastor a bit the night before. Well, she had. Amanda had pretty much dominated the conversation as Finn loosened up and remembered what it was like to talk to a beautiful woman.

He hadn't been great at it, but he felt he could improve, with enough time and practice. He felt younger than he had in years as the phone rang. He fiddled with his knot still, something about it not right. But he couldn't devote full brain power to fixing it, because he was calling Amanda Whittaker.

His heart raced faster with every second she didn't pick up. The call finally ended, and he hung up before her voicemail message started.

A moment later, his phone buzzed in his hand, cutting through the disappointment raging through him. *In church,* Amanda said. *I'll call you later?*

Mine starts in a half an hour, he messaged back, his thumbs feeling thick and slow.

Maybe I could bring you lunch, she said, and Finn's breath burst from his body.

Sure, his sausage-fingers typed out. *Not spending today with your family?*

She'd mentioned the lodge up the west canyon, and when she spoke of her sons, their wives and families, it was clear she loved them deeply. Finn had liked that. Liked the enthusiasm family sparked in her.

He didn't see his daughters much, and he had no reason to talk to Holly anymore. But he loved Kimberly and Joann, and he did talk to them, text them, and stay in touch with them regularly. Neither of them was interested in breeding and training racehorses, but Finn hadn't been able to give up his boarding stable, tuck his tail, and return to Nashville.

He wouldn't.

He didn't need his father's power and prestige. He was doing just fine selling to the rich and famous on his own. Of course, his last name helped.

It had been too long for him to return to the family farms in Nashville anyway. He'd been gone for thirty-five years, and grudges ran deep in the South.

Amanda hadn't answered his question, and he would be late for church if he didn't get going. So he banished thoughts of his father to the back of his mind, took off his tie and re-tied it, and headed out the door, hoping he hadn't upset Amanda by asking her about her family.

After all, he really had no idea how to date at age fifty-five, with a bruised heart and his whole life wrapped up in horses that ate better meals than he did.

HER COWBOY BILLIONAIRE BLIND DATE, featuring Amanda Whittaker and the man she allows her sons to set her up with, is now available! **You can read it in paperback right now.**

Keep scrolling to view series starters from three of my other series!

IVORY PEAKS ROMANCE SERIES

Experience true Rocky Mountain life in the Ivory Peaks Romance series! You'll get more Hammond family romance, second chance romance, and all the heartwarming and uplifting family fiction you're craving. Ivory Peaks is the perfect escape for anyone looking to feel loved, cherished, and like they belong. You belong right here in Ivory Peaks!

His First Love (Book 1): She broke up with him a decade ago. He's back in town after finishing a degree at MIT, ready to start his job at the family company. **Can Hunter and Molly find their way through their pasts to build a future together?**

SEVEN SONS RANCH IN THREE RIVERS ROMANCE SERIES

Meet the cowboy billionaire brothers at Seven Sons Ranch. The Walkers are new in Three Rivers, and they've got the women circling. Every contemporary romance in this series features a fake marriage that turns to more, family holiday traditions, and the family saga that will create a space for you in the Walker family too!

Rhett's Make-Believe Marriage (Book 1): To save her business, she'll have to risk her heart. She needs a husband to be credible as a matchmaker. He wants to help a neighbor. **Will their fake marriage take them out of the friend zone?**

STEEPLE RIDGE ROMANCE SERIES

Get cowboy brothers working together at a horse farm in beautiful Vermont in the Steeple Ridge Farm romance series! With sweet, clean, and faith-filled western romance in a complete series, you'll get a cowboy billionaire, friends to lovers romance, holiday romance, and second chance romance with fun and unique plots (aquaponics, anyone?).

Her Billionaire Cowboy (Book 1): Tucker Jenkins has had enough of tall buildings, traffic, and has traded in his technology firm in New York City for Steeple Ridge Horse Farm in rural Vermont. Missy Marino has worked at the farm since she was a teen, and she's always dreamed of owning it. But her ex-husband left her with a truckload of debt, making her fantasies of owning the farm unfulfilled. Tucker didn't come to the country to find a new wife, but he supposes a woman could help him start over in Steeple Ridge. Will Tucker and Missy be able to navigate the shaky ground between them to find a new beginning?

ABOUT LIZ

Liz Isaacson writes inspirational romance, usually set in Texas, or Wyoming, or anywhere else horses and cowboys exist. She lives in Utah, where she writes full-time, takes her two dogs to the park everyday, and eats a lot of veggies while writing. Find her on her website, along with all of her pen names, at feelgood-fictionbooks.com

www.ingramcontent.com/pod-product-compliance
Lightning Source LLC
Chambersburg PA
CBHW021959130726
47903CB00014B/2499